WHAT THE BARBER KNEW

A David Elliott Mystery

BAILEY HERRINGTON

More Beyond Books

To Karen Dumont, my wife and best friend,
who encourages me to see life as opportunity.

If a little knowledge is dangerous,
where is the man who has so much knowledge
as to be out of danger?

THOMAS HUXLEY

CHAPTER 1

David Sees His Barber

For six years I've been expecting my life would change any day, and for the better. For a whole lot better. Today I learned that it wouldn't. Still, I can't help thinking about it - what happened, and what should have happened instead.

It all started when my mother asked me to go to the store for ice cream. I was reading the Sports Page of the Erie Daily Times, checking on the Pirates and Braves game from the day before. They lost again. Why the heck did they get Murry Dickson from the Cards? He gives up more hits than an amateur boxer fighting Rocky Marciano. Geez, it was the middle of June and the Bucs hadn't won twenty games yet.

"David Elliott, I need you here in the kitchen. Right now."

Shoot. Now what? I tossed the paper on the coffee table and went into the kitchen. Mother was in a foul mood. Hands on hips, a wooden spoon clenched in one fist, she stood in front of the refrigerator. Someone had eaten the remainder of the butter pecan ice cream she intended for dessert. Nobody confessed, but Mother, as usual, blamed my sister, Jeannie, who was fighting early-teen blarpiness. Mother was always on her case about being overweight.

I hate to admit it, but because Mother's criticism was aimed at Jeannie most of the time, I - and Jimmy - got away with a lot of stuff. In retrospect, I understand Mother's attitude. She could have handled Jeannie with more sensitivity, yes. However, women in the 1950s didn't have many options for careers. Secretaries, nurses, teachers. That was about it. Mother figured - and she wasn't alone in her thinking - that the best chance Jeannie or any young woman had for happiness in life pointed in one direction: get married to a good man, have two or three kids, and live in a nice house in the suburbs. And I think Mother believed Jeannie's best chance to realize that dream required her to be slim and attractive, not with a body Rubens liked to paint. I'm not justifying Mother's treatment of Jeannie then, but she wanted the best for her daughter and that seemed to be the only way to achieve it.

From my vantage point as the teenage older brother, I noticed the more Mother criticized Jeannie, the more candy and French fries she ate. I shared my observation with Jeannie one afternoon when she was working on a bag of potato chips. At dumped the potato chips on my head and told me to mind my own business. Hindsight is always 20/20 as the saying goes. Now that I'm in my twenties, I look back and see my family dynamics from a longer view. Since then I've learned that Mother's parents were basically tyrants. She had to be perfect in every way, every minute. Mother never told me this. Her brother did. On top of this, she was worried about Dad's health. He worked too darn hard, and he smoked too many cigarettes. He still doesn't take enough time off to do what he loves best: to putter around in his garden.

Just listen to me, the self-appointed family counselor. That's what a college course in psychology will do to you. Anyway, on that particular day I doubted Jeannie had emptied the ice cream container. Personally, I suspected Jimmy, my little brother. Last week I watched Jimmy scarf down about a pint of homemade applesauce and leave the empty jar in the fridge. It was the same thing with the ice cream–the empty carton was sitting on the freezer shelf.

"David, take the car and go to Strubles for a quart of butter pecan. Your dad's on a long distance call with his boss." She opened her purse and handed me some money. As I walked toward the back door, Jimmy grinned at me, a smirky, shitty smile. I stopped. He darted out of the room. Should I . . . oh, the heck with it.

That's why I was driving Dad's company car to Strubles Drug Store to rescue Mother's dessert plans. Ordinarily I would have walked to Strubles. It's no more than a couple of blocks. But this was sort of an emergency. Dad likes to have supper over and done with early so he can get out in his garden and check on his crops while there's still some daylight left.

It's funny how things happen sometimes. If Jimmy hadn't eaten the ice cream, then I wouldn't have seen Dolores Cooper walking along Sanford Place. Dolores and I are going steady. I rolled down the side window and pulled to the curb.

"Hi, Dolores. Need a lift?" Dolores was a peach.

Short blonde hair, a body like Brigit Bardot, a terrific smile, and lips so soft they always seemed ready. She wears glasses, but she takes them off when we're making out. Dolores climbed in and slid over to my side of the front seat. My mission to buy ice cream melted right out of my brain when Dolores's bare leg squeezed up against me. She kissed me on the ear, and before I knew what I was doing, I drove down to Sonnhalter's deserted lake house. The house was up on a cliff that overlooked the lake, and around the back of it there's a secluded parking spot.

The house has been vacant since Mrs. Sonnhalter died three years ago. Her grandson, Bill, used to stay at her house during the summer. Bill was kind of wild . He was a daredevil. Bill wasn't afraid to try anything. We used to climb along the cliffs in back of her house, walking on the narrow shale ledges, holding the ledge above for balance. It was scary. Those cliffs are probably thirty or forty feet high. A fall from that height could kill you. We had some close calls.

As I turned the car into the lane next to Sonnhalter's, I noticed a car parked at the bottom of the hill on Lakeside Drive. Probably some guy checking gauges at the pumping station. Whoever it was wouldn't be able to see us.

Things had just started to heat up when Dolores pulled away, her cute nose wrinkling. "God," she said, which really surprised me because Dolores never says *God*. "What stinks?" After I broke away from the daze Dolores's kisses always cause, I smelled it too. Death.

"It's probably a dead woodchuck or something."
I attempted a return to the business at hand. Time was running out: I had to get the ice cream before Strubles closed.

But Dolores decided she had to see the corpse. Oh, for crying out loud! We hadn't walked far into the bushes before we saw the fawn, lying on its side, blow flies rising from its belly.

"Let's go back to the car," I said. I didn't have much more time to be with Dolores.

She took my hand. "In a minute. Let's walk back there through the honeysuckle bushes; see what it's like." We made our way beyond the vines into an overgrown grassy place. You couldn't see the lake. In fact, you couldn't see anything beyond the surrounding bushes and trees. Far below us the lazy lake water sloshed through the narrow gravel beach, like root beer swirling through finely crushed ice.

"Come here, David," she whispered. She began to disrobe. I was closing my gaping mouth just as she kissed me. She spread her blouse and shorts on the grass, sat, and stretched out full length. "Come here," Dolores repeated, lifting her arms. I was so excited, I pulled off the top button of my fly. Shoot! Where the heck did it go? How am I gonna explain that particular missing button to my mother? I looked at Dolores, aroused by her naked body. In seconds I stripped off my shirt and pushed my jeans and boxers to my ankles. I knelt over the beautiful and willing Dolores.

That's when I saw it.

Just a couple yards behind her blonde hair and

shining blue eyes, I saw a man's hand on the ground, half-hidden by leaves and weeds. I sprang backward, falling away and scrabbling to my feet, I yanked up my shorts and jeans.

"What?"

"Get up! We gotta get outta here! Someone's lying in the weeds! A guy! I think he's dead!"

Dolores rolled over, saw the fingers and screamed. She snatched up her clothes, bent, and shoved on her shoes. I grabbed her hand and we ran. At the edge of the underbrush, I stopped. Dolores crouched behind me, hastily pulling on her clothes. The car was about twenty yards away. I didn't see or hear anything unusual, although my ragged breathing probably drowned out any other sounds. Inside the car, Dolores grabbed my arm like a drowning person grabs a tree branch. "God! Oh my God!" She was trembling.

"Stay here. I'm going back to take a look." I'm no hero. But I wasn't gonna toss my cookies in front of Dolores.

Geez, I was shaking so badly I could hardly put one foot in front of the other. I stood above the hand for a few seconds until my breathing slowed. Stooping, I parted the weeds with quavering fingers. The man was on his back, a black hole in his face beneath his left eye. Both eyes were open really wide, like he saw something coming at him and couldn't get out of the way in time, sort of like the face batters make when Sammy Williamson throws a fastball at their heads. Then it hit me. *Cripes! It's Mr. Angelone! Benny*

Angelone, my barber! I nearly puked on his foot. Someone murdered my barber! But why? Did he give the wrong type of guy a bad haircut?

A twig snapped over to my right. My heart started thumping so fast I thought I was having a heart attack. The tangled honeysuckle vines kept me from seeing anything. But since I was standing next to the body, the killer, if the killer had caused the sound, sure as heck knew where I was. Before I got shot I had to warn Dolores. *She could drive the car to escape . . . no, she couldn't. The car key was in my pocket.* Dead leaves crackled. A squirrel scampered into view. Let me tell you, I've never been so happy to see a stupid squirrel.

The car horn sounded. Dolores! Oh my Gosh! I dashed back to her. She was OK, if wringing her hands is a sign of being OK.

"It's Mr. Angelone, the barber up on Euclid. Someone shot him."

"Let's get out of here!" she pleaded, tucking her blouse into her shorts. "Mother's gonna kill me."

I backed out fast, not doing a good job of it, smacking into bushes, bumping over a rock. As we drove along Lakeside, Dolores stared straight ahead, her body shivering. "Why did I let you give me a ride?"

"What?!"

"If you hadn't come along, I'd be home right now and none of this would have happened to me."

"Geez, Dolores, you wanted to make out as much as I did." *Maybe more*, I thought, but I had the brains not to say so. "Listen. We have to figure out what to do. We need to call the police and…"

7

"What? Tell them we were about to have sex behind Sonnhalter's?"

"No, of course not. We could just say we decided to look at the lake, see if there were any ore boats or something. But we gotta report it. Cripes, someone murdered my barber!"

"Well, he's not going anywhere. Let someone else find the body and report it."

"Look, Dolores, Mr. Angelone must've been shot not long before we got there. He was still sorta warm."

"You touched him!?"

"All I'm saying is whoever did it could still be nearby, waiting for us to leave. I read a lot of detective novels, and they all make the same point: the sooner the police and forensic experts get to the scene of the crime, the better the chance the murderer will be caught."

"Can the lecture, will you? Get going!"

We drove in silence the entire five minutes to Cooper's driveway. "You okay, Dolores?" I asked as she was getting out. She shot me a look that said, you have to be kidding.

"David, I'm going to tell my parents that you picked me up and asked me to go for a ride out to GE to deliver a package for your Dad or something. It's full of holes, but it's the best excuse I can think of." She shook her head. "I'm gonna have nightmares about this." She leaned toward me, her eyes fixed on mine. "Please, if you love me, don't get us involved in this."

I wanted to kiss her, but sure as heck her

mother would be watching from behind the living room curtains. Dolores touched my hand on the wheel.

"I think it would be smart if we didn't see each other for a while. I do love you David." Then she slipped out of the car and ran into the house.

As I drove to Strubles for ice cream, my mind ping-ponged back and forth. Should I tell the truth and call the police or lie to Mother and Dad? Dolores sort of had a good point. Mr. Angelone wasn't going anywhere. But the tire tracks in that lane were from Dad's car: could the police somehow trace those tracks? That seemed like a long shot. What about that car parked down by the pumping station? Was it still there when we zoomed out onto Lakeside? I had absolutely no idea. But if that car was there and the driver saw how fast I was driving, would he take special notice of the make and model of the car and tell the cops when the murder was discovered? Well, maybe the make and model, but it would be too far away to read the license number, and there are tons of black 1950 Ford two-doors on the streets.

Wait a minute! What if that car belonged to the killer? My heart raced. *Calm down, Elliott. No car had followed us.* But what if the murderer had been hiding near the body when we got there? He probably would have shot us. So maybe he wasn't nearby. The more I thought about it, the more mixed up I got. Sonnhalter's was a popular necking spot, and Mr.Weinbrenner used the old stone steps behind the house 'most every day to get down to the lakeshore. So the odds were pretty good someone would find Mr. Angelone by to-morrow, or the next day at the latest.

So, I made up my mind not to call the cops. I would make up a story for Dad and Mother. I'm not saying that was the right thing to do, 'cause it wasn't, but I was nuts about Dolores and didn't want anything to come between us, namely our parents. If my parents (especially my mother) and the Coopers learned that we were about to go all the way just before we found the body (and I couldn't see how they wouldn't if we had to tell the police what we were doing back there in the bushes), you can bet your last buck they would have forbidden us to see each other again.

Okay, I just had to decide what story would sound less fishy–that Strubles shut early for some reason, and I had to drive to East Avenue to get butter pecan (Ernie's Red and White Store didn't carry Gem City butter pecan,) or, that I came upon a guy whose car broke down and he needed a ride to Hamot Hospital to have a doctor stitch the cut on his kid's leg...

Strubles was open, and Mr. Strubles had one quart of Gem City butter pecan left. Back home, I parked the car in the driveway. Dad was waiting for me at the back door. "Sorry, I'm late. A guy had his car break down on Sanford and he stopped me and asked if I could take him and his kid to Hamot. His kid had a nasty cut on his leg. So, I thought you'd want me to help." Dad seemed to buy it. "Here's the ice cream. I got the last of the butter pecan." Mother was looking at me queerly. *Shoot! The top button on my fly!* Had she seen it was gone?

"Jeannie," she said to my sister, "will you please dish out the ice cream? Or maybe you've already had enough butter pecan ice cream. If so, just do three dishes."

"I didn't eat that ice cream. Why can't you believe me?" Jeannie wailed. Mother ignored her.

Dad stood at the kitchen window, looking at his garden as he often did. No kidding, Dad could see tomato hornworms munching on his plants at twenty yards. But he wasn't watching for tomato worms. He turned back from the window.

"That was a good thing you did, Dave. We all need to help those who are in trouble." With the most innocent look on his face, Dad asked, "What road did you take to the hospital?"

Uh-oh.

"Uh, Lake Road to State at Public Square, right on State, then I drove right up to the Emergency Room door." I swallowed hard.

"Ah. So, have they planted bushes in the middle of State Street? Or did you detour through a field to dodge the mud puddles on Lake Road?"

Mother, Jeannie, and Jimmy stopped all activity and watched the scene. Jeannie knew I was lying. She was always telling Mother that I lied.

"Huh?" I croaked.

"There's a leafy branch stuck to the right rear fender. Mud splashes too."

"What on earth?" Mother exclaimed, moving to the window. I wanted to wipe the smirk off Jeannie's fat face. "The truth, young man. No more of your lies."

"Okay, but I want to tell you what happened in private."

"In private?" said Mother. "Now you listen to..."

But Dad heard the undertone of fear in my voice. He told Jeannie and Jimmy to take their ice cream dishes upstairs and close their bedroom doors.

I recited most of the truth, leaving out the circumstances just before I spotted Mr. Angelone's hand. I hoped it would be enough to protect Dolores and myself from parent wrath and the certain breakup of our love affair.

Needless to say, they were horrified. Mother was sure the killer was going to come after me, which Dad said was unlikely since Dolores and I hadn't seen anyone. Mother blamed Dolores for persuading me to take her to the lake instead of coming right home from Strubles.

"If she hadn't worked her charms on you this wouldn't have happened."

"Wait a minute," I began, "I was the one who persuaded Dolores..."

"That's enough you two," Dad broke in. "This isn't the time to bicker. Jimmy and Jeannie are going to hear about this eventually. Em, will you go up and tell them a sanitized version? We don't want Jimmy to have nightmares." Then Dad phoned the police.

That night two detectives from the Erie police department knocked on our front door.

"Good evening, Mr. Elliott," said the short, pudgy one. "I'm Detective Sergeant Joe Pelinski, and this is my partner, Roland Washington." He and Washington, who was bald, showed Dad their badges. "We understand…"

"Please excuse me for interrupting, Detective Pelinski," said Dad, "but I need to clear the room. Jeannie, turn off the television set and take Jimmy up to your rooms." Ordinarily there would have been a protest about missing the rest of Kukla, Fran, and Ollie, but not tonight.

When they reached the second floor, the detective resumed speaking. "We understand David had the unpleasant experience of discovering the body of his barber, Mr. Angelone, late this afternoon. Detective Washington and I have just finished our search of the crime scene, and we need to ask your son some questions."

"Yes, sure," said Dad. "Please, sit down. This is David." I had been standing in the entryway between the living room and the dining room while all this was taking place. Geez, I was sweating like a pig on account of being nervous. When they introduced themselves, I wiped my sweaty palms on my dungarees, but neither of them shook my hand.

"Mr. and Mrs. Elliott," Detective Pelinski said, "We need to talk with your son alone. Do you mind?"

Dad asked, "Why alone?"

"It's not required, and of course you may remain if you wish. But it's been our experience as police officers that teenagers remember more when parents aren't in the room." Dad and Mother exchanged a look then retreated up the stairs.

When we were alone, they sat on the and I grabbed a dining room chair. They asked lots of questions about what I had seen, but nothing about why Dolores and I were parked there. They knew why. Detective Washington went outside to examine Dad's car by flashlight. He reminded me of the two black men I worked with on my summer job on the labor gang at Perry Iron, Shorty and Willie. In fact, Willie's last name was Washington. Willie and Shorty were great locker room buddies. They taught me some clever ways to keep my clothes from being covered in iron ore dust, and when Willie taught me the best way to sledge open an ore car hopper, my work got a heck of a lot easier.

Detective Pelinski kept asking me about what I had seen and what I had heard. He copied my answers in a little notebook he balanced on his knee as he wrote.

"Did you see anyone before or after you found Mr. Angelone?"

"No, sir."

"Did you or your companion attempt to move the body?

"No, sir"

"About how long were you and your companion at that place before you discovered the body?"

"Uh, not long."

Pelinski wasn't satisfied. "Can you be more specific? "Two minutes? Five?"

14

"I'd say it was more like ten minutes."

He looked up from his notes and gave me this smirky smile to let me know he got the picture. Detective Washington opened the front door and returned to the living room. Pelinski looked at him.

"Nothing significant," said Washington, sitting on the sofa. Pelinski continued the questions. "Did you ever see anyone in the barbershop who wasn't there to get a shave or a haircut?"

"Well, there have been times when a guy would come in and Mr. Angelone would stop cutting hair and take him into a back room, which I think is where Mr. Angelone lived. They wouldn't stay very long. When they came out, the guy would leave, and Mr. Angelone would get back to work. As a matter of fact, last Saturday while I was waiting to get a haircut there was a guy, stocky build, talking with Mr. Angelone in the back room. I couldn't really hear what about, though. The door was closed."

"Yeah," Detective Washington cut in, "we know Mr. Angelone operated another business from his shop."

Detective Pelinski closed his book and stuffed it in the inside pocket of his suit.

"I think that'll do for tonight. Sorry you had to be the one to find Mr. Angelone." He and Washington stood at the exact same moment. "Mr. And Mrs. Elliott?" Pelinski called up the stairs, "We're leaving." Dad and Mother came down. "David, we'd like you to come to the police station tomorrow morning to look at some photos. Maybe you'll recognize someone you saw at the barber shop. OK?

"Sure," said Dad. "We'll be there sometime after breakfast."

As they were leaving, Detective Washington asked me to go out on the front porch with him. He pressed something into my hand. A spool of navy blue thread, the color of a police uniform and the button. "Here, kid. Learn how to sew on a button before your mother notices." They both chuckled. I didn't think anything about this was funny at all.

CHAPTER 2

Pictures, Pictures

The next morning, the atmosphere inside the house was definitely below freezing. Mother busied herself scrambling eggs while Dad read the *Erie Daily Times*. The front page headlined the conflict between the Electrical Workers' Union and GE. Dad had scoured the entire paper. Mr. Angelone's murder hadn't been reported in time for the morning edition. A lucky break. Dolores's parents didn't know anything yet, I figured.

"Jeannie, did you butter the toast? These eggs are ready."

"Yep."

"Don't say 'yep'. How many times have I told you kids to use correct English?"

"Yes, Mother, the toast is buttered,"

We might as well have eaten breakfast in a monastery, what with the lack of conversation around the table. The only noise came from Jimmy chewing with his mouth open. If Jeannie or I had done that, we would have been told to leave the room until we remembered our table manners. Dad folded the paper and swallowed the last of his coffee. He pushed back his chair and stood.

"You finished, Dave? It's time to go."

"Yeah - I mean, yes."

"Where you going?" Jimmy asked.

"None of your beeswax," I said, which earned me a brief scolding from Dad.

Erie Police Headquarters was twenty minutes away by car. I wanted to ask Dad what the procedure would be at the police station, but a quick sideways glance at his clenched jaw persuaded me to keep my mouth shut. He pulled into a parking space and shut off the engine. Then Dad told me Mr. Cooper had called him before I came down for breakfast. The detectives had visited Dolores last night, too. From what Dad said, I got the impression Mr. Cooper was really steamed that his daughter had lied, but also shook up that she had been so close to a murder victim. *Yeah*, I thought, *if you only knew how close.*

"Look," Dad said as we sat on a bench outside the Detective Bureau office, "I'm not mad at you for parking with Dolores. I probably would have done the same thing at your age. But you were wrong to lie about it. You should have reported the killing right away. Maybe the delay won't make it tougher to catch the killer, but maybe it will. I've told you a thousand times it's always better to tell the truth."

The office door opened and Detective Washington motioned us in. The other detective, Sergeant Pelinski, sat behind a beat-up steel desk piled high with papers and a couple of coffee-stained cups.

"Thanks for coming in," said Pelinski. "Before we have you look at our family photo albums, Detective Washington and I have a few more questions for you, David."

The questions were mostly the same ones they had asked me the night before. Stuff like–how much time would you say elapsed before you returned to look at the victim? Was that your vomit near the victim's right foot? When was the last time you saw Mr. Angelone alive? Anything else you can think of, any little detail you might have forgotten?

Geez! The car parked by the pumping station! "When we got to the track that goes behind the Sonnhalter place, there was a black Cadillac down at the bottom of the hill on Lakeside in front of the pumping station by Two-Mile Creek. Sorry, I forgot to mention it." The detectives looked at each other. Washington asked if it was still parked there when we left, but I had been concentrating on getting out of there and hadn't noticed.

"That's okay, kid," Washington assured me. "You're sure it was a Cadillac?" I nodded. "What year?"

"1950." Like every teenager, I knew makes and models of cars.

"Did you see anyone inside the car, or maybe standing outside?"

"No sir, nobody." I was sure of it, because I didn't want any neighbors to see me drive to Sonnhalter's make-out spot. I knew nobody in the neighborhood drove a new Caddy.

"Okay, David, let's go back into the file room where you can look at some mug shots," Washington said. "Mr. Elliott, I'll get you a cup of battery acid, also known as coffee, although it bears no resemblance to any coffee you've ever had. You can wait for David in the hall."

"That's fine," Dad replied. "Listen, are David and Dolores in any danger? I mean, would the killer figure they may have seen him and come after them?"

Detective Washington put his hand on Dad's shoulder. "No, sir, I doubt it. Of course, you can never be 100 percent sure in these situations."

Oh, great, I thought. *Just what is the percentage of certainty in these situations?"*

Dad looked skeptical. Pelinski chimed in, "Since neither David nor Miss Cooper actually saw the crime being committed, and saw nobody before or after, it's unlikely their lives are in jeopardy."

Dad remained dissatisfied. "But what if the killer thinks they saw something incriminating? Wouldn't he want to make sure they couldn't identify him?"

"Mr. Elliott," Pelinski said in a kind of patronizing way, "I know this is all new to you and your family. Naturally, You're a bit worried. But we're trained to deal with this sort of thing. If we thought your son and his friend were in danger, I guarantee the Erie Police Department would take necessary action. Do you take milk and sugar in your coffee?" Conversation closed. The limp reassurance wasn't doing much to make me feel any safer.

While Dad waited in the hall, the detectives walked me into another room and had me sit at a long table. From the wall of shelves, Detective Washington pulled out a big thick 3-ring binder. "Okay, David, take your time and look carefully at every photo. If you see anyone you recognize or even someone you think looks familiar, point him out. Want something to drink? Coke? Water?"

"No, sir. Thank you." I turned to the first page. They were front-view and side-view black-and-white photos. Mostly men, but there were two women, too. Neither looked like types you'd bring home to meet your folks. Beneath the photos were dates and numbers. One of the guys looked like he was already dead. And there was one guy who was smiling, a wide all-the -teeth smile as if someone had slipped him a hacksaw baked in a chocolate cake.

On about the tenth page, there was a photo of a guy I had seen more than once sitting in Angelone's Barber Shop. His black hair was shiny-slick, as though he used motor oil for hair cream. Beneath bushy black eyebrows his eyes had this look—kind of like he was always daring someone to knock the chip off his shoulder. Mike "Fat Stuff" Budzik was his name. Born April 11, 1919. I motioned to Detective Washington.

"This guy isn't the man who was talking to Mr. Angelone last Saturday, but he's been in the barber shop a couple of times when I was there," I said. "Both times he just sat, never said anything, and even though he was there before me, he never got a haircut."

"You're sure, David? Look again. We need you to be absolutely sure." I looked again. From the list of crimes he'd been committed, "Fat Stuff" wasn't a person I'd want to identify mistakenly. After studying Mike Budzik's face, I said, "Yeah, that's him."

"Good work," Washington clapped me on the shoulder. "Budzik has a bad temper. One time he stomped a guy to death in Cleveland because he'd been cheated out of sixty bucks. Budzik got off scot-free due to some legal technicality. Not a good citizen."

Holy cow! I had been sitting in the same room with a killer who got away with murder! If Detective Washington said that to scare me, it worked. My fear meter zoomed upward to near panic. If I had recognized "Fat Stuff" Budzik, chances are he could recognize me.

"We want you to keep looking. Maybe you'll recognize that guy you heard talking to Benny, or someone else you remember from Angelone's." It took me more than an hour to finish. The stocky guy from last Saturday was not among the faces in any of the books. Geez, there are lots of crooks out there.

As Dad and I walked down the outside steps to the parking lot, a man dressed in a brown suit and Fedora walked up. He was younger than Dad and wore glasses and a phony smile. "Excuse me for bothering you. My name's Tom Eldred. I'm a reporter for the *Daily Times*. David, I understand you were the one who discovered the body of Mr. Angelone, the murdered man." And before we knew what was going on, another guy came up and took my picture, and the reporter started asking a bunch of questions. "What were you doing behind the Sonnhalter house? What did you do after you saw the corpse? Did you see any . . ."

Dad got in his face. "Beat it. We're not answering any of your damn questions, and if you publish that picture, I'll sue. You hear me? Now get out of our way." He pushed Eldred in the chest and we climbed into the car. I couldn't believe Dad said damn! He had handled those two in a way that clearly said he wasn't someone to monkey with. Proud, that's what I was.

He rammed the Ford into first and darn near peeled rubber leaving the lot. "Listen, David, and listen good. Don't talk about this business with anyone. You've put your finger on a dangerous man. You've connected him with Benny Angelone. Maybe there's nothing to it, but nevertheless, you saw him in Angelone's not more than two weeks ago. No telling what he might do if he knew who you are and where you live. Do I make myself clear?"

"Yes, Dad." What he said scared me. But the more I thought about it, the more the fear began to fade away. After all, neither Dolores nor I had seen anybody. Granted, we weren't exactly focused on our surroundings, but a guy as big as Mike Budzik would've been pretty easy to spot. And if he wasn't there, how would he ever find out it was me and Dolores who found the body?

Then a question occurred to me; how did that reporter know my name and that I had found the body? Someone in the police department must have tipped him off. That's just great. If my picture got printed in the paper, there was a really good chance the killer then would know for sure who to go after. Besides, this was a very serious matter to cause Dad to utter the word "*damn*." He was the son of starchy

Methodists who punished swearing with a mouthful of soap. Dad had eight brothers and sisters, all of whom smoked and drank lots of beer, but never in GrandMother and GrandDad Elliott's presence.

Dad let me out of the car at Euclid and East Lake Road, two blocks from the house. He still had sales calls to make, and the GE plant was out east on Lake. My thoughts turned to Dolores. I needed to see her and talk with her, make sure she was okay, especially was she still okay with me. Baseball practice wasn't until 3:30 that afternoon, so I figured I'd walk through Mr. Chopka's yard and pay Dolores a visit.

Dolores was home alone. Both her mother and father worked uptown. So did her older sister, Judy. On the few occasions when I took time to observe Judy and Mrs. Cooper, I caught a glimpse of what Dolores would look like at different points in her future, both in her 20s and when she got really old like her mother. It wasn't a bad prospect, actually. Both Judy and her mother were pretty good looking. You can usually rely on family resemblances in that way, although my cousin Ruthie is an exception. My Dad's sister, Velma, would not have won any beauty contests, but her daughter, Ruthie, is a knockout.

Dolores let me in the side door. She kissed me, which took a load off my mind, believe you me. She had forgotten her remark about not seeing each other.

"Thanks for not saying anything about us," she said. "I really love you, David."

"I love you, too." We sat on the living room sofa, holding hands. Dolores was wearing those short shorts her mother forbade her to wear in public, which was okay, 'cause none of the other wolves got to see what I got to see. I described my morning at the police station, including the encounter with the reporter from the paper. Dad had told me not to talk about it, but Dolores was with me at the scene of the crime. Why shouldn't she get the details?

Dolores put her head on my shoulder. "Please, please, be careful. I don't want anything to happen to you."

"Nothin's gonna happen to me," I said. "Fat Stuff doesn't scare me. Besides, he may not have had anything to do with the murder. Just because he was in the barber shop a couple of times doesn't necessarily mean anything."

"My father says you're dangerous and I should break up with you." She laughed. "Goodness, if he only knew how dangerous."

"What did you say to him?"

"That I'll make up my own mind about my friends, that you always treat me with respect, and that I'm happy when we're together."

It was everything I needed to hear. I tried to pick up where we left off in back of Sonnhalter's, but Dolores closed the door on that plan pretty quick. We talked about some things going on with our friends; so and so broke up with her boyfriend; Darlene, one of our high school's baton twirlers, fell off her bike and broke her elbow.

"I gotta get goin', sweetheart. What about Friday night? Do you think your father will let you have the car?" Dolores and I had a date Friday to see the movie, *Young Man With A Horn.* My parents didn't own a car then. Dad was a salesman for The Hickman Steel Company out of Pittsburgh and they gave him a company car to drive. No one else, not even mother, was supposed to drive the black Ford unless it was an emergency, (like going to Strubles for Gem City butter pecan.) That eventful little trip would mark the last of my driving for a good long time. Dolores replied that today was not the day to ask her father for the car because he and her mother were upset about us stumbling onto a corpse. Her plan was to wait 'til Friday and spring it on him. If he nixed the idea, maybe she or I could persuade one of our Dads to drive us. If that were the case, I hoped it would be Mr. Cooper. He never looked in his rearview mirror, a fact Dolores and I had discovered from the back seat on a three-hour trip home from Letchworth Park on Memorial Day.

Baseball practice was a big waste. Mr. Munch was a better Physics teacher than he was a baseball coach, and that's not saying much. But we had two pretty good pitchers and some solid hitters, and we were tied for first place with Cathedral Prep. Thursday night we had a game with Prep, but Gil, as everybody called Coach Munch, conducted a pretty lackadaisy practice. None of the guys except Bobby Russell seemed fired up and ready to play. I was the best hitter on the squad, and I didn't even hit a loud foul in batting practice. My head was elsewhere. All I could think of was Mr. Angelone lying there with his eyes open and that bullet hole in his cheek.

When Mel Cabeloff dropped an easy pop-up behind second, then laughed about it, Gil just said kind of indifferently, "C'mon, Mel. Use both hands." Cabeloff was good, but not as good as he thought he was. If we didn't play better than this on Thursday, Prep was going to wipe the field with us. When practice ended, Coach Munch had us sit on the grass behind first base.

"Okay, boys," he began, clapping his hands for emphasis, "you know Thursday's game is big. Prep is a very good team. The winner will stand alone in first place, okay?" Gil used *okay* in just about every sentence. "Now, look-it, Sammy Williamson will pitch for them. I don't have to tell you boys he's their ace. His fastball is the best in this state." I glanced at Ronnie Lukasheski, our best hurler. Ronnie had a fast ball every bit as good as Sammy's. He just looked down at the grass.

Prep's hitters are dangerous, especially Cesar Montoya. What's he got? Twelve home runs?"

Way to go, Gil, I thought, *nothing like a good pep talk to get us fired up.* I hoped he was using reverse psychology, that pretty soon he'd say we can't possibly win a game against this Prep powerhouse. That there was no use trying. "You kids don't measure up talent-wise." That sort of thing.

And we'd respond, "the heck we can't beat them! We'll show you, Gil!"

"Okay," Coach continued, clapping his hands signifying the pep talk was finished, "We play the second game Thursday, so you need to be at the field by 7:00. Meanwhile, don't do anything I wouldn't," he winked at Cabeloff. That was it. *Reverse psychology my foot.*

The headline on the morning edition of the *Daily Times* read "LOCAL BARBER SLAIN!" Tom Eldred had reported all the gory details, but I wasn't reading the story. My eyes stared at the photograph of my face on the front page. "David Elliott, son of Mr. and Mrs. Harold Elliott, discovered the body," stated the caption. *Swell. Dad's phone number and address were in the city phonebook. How many Harold Elliotts lived in Erie? Not many, I bet. Unless he was dumber than a fence post, Mr. Angelone's killer could easily find out where I lived. Not good.*

Dad's office door was closed, but I had no trouble hearing him reaming out someone. The phone slammed. Dad flung back the door and tore into the kitchen. Jimmy paused with a spoonful of Wheaties halfway between the bowl and his open mouth. Vesuvius was about to erupt.

"Jeannie," Dad's calm voice not jibing with the set of his jaw, "I want you and Jimmy to go out on the front porch."

Jimmy protested. "But I'm not finished eating my cereal."

"Right now, mister." When Jimmy heard Dad address him as *mister*, he high-tailed it to the porch. You could always tell how bad you were in for it by the personal noun Dad and Mother used. *Mister* or *Sister* meant no further words would be allowed from whichever one of us was in the spotlight. We'd better do what Dad or Mother wanted right away or else. Just a trifle lower on the trouble scale, we were called by our full given names. "David Arthur, come here this instant." A lesser offense warranted "David," As in, "David, how many times must I tell you not to throw the tennis ball against the garage door?" We knew the code.

When they were out of earshot, Dad told Mother and me that the managing editor of the paper had made no apology for publishing my picture, saying the murder was the biggest news story in Erie since the sinking of The Simon Steele off Presque Isle in 1931. According to him, *The Times* had an obligation to the citizens to print the whole truth, and so on.

"Harold, You're getting too upset," Mother cautioned. "Think of your blood pressure." Dad lit a cigarette. He smoked a lot in those days. So did Mother.

"Listen," he said. "This thing isn't going to fade away until the newspapers are satisfied that they can't get any new information from you, Dave. I repeat: keep your lip buttoned. Don't talk to anyone and maybe people will forget your role in this."

"Okay, Dad."

"Em," Dad looked at Mother, "If anyone from the paper calls, hang up."

"Alright," she said. "And while we're in the middle of this, I don't think Dave and Dolores should go to the movie Friday, dear. People will see Dave and start asking questions."

"We can't crawl into a shell, Em. Dave can handle this." *Yeah, Mother*, I was thinking, *don't have a cow.*

"Why do you always blame everything on Dolores? You and Dad should be glad I'm dating her and not some of the girls I know about."

"That's enough, Dave."

"No, let me finish." I looked at Mother. "I feel like you don't trust me, that you still think of me as a little boy. I don't cause you any trouble, at least not until now. My grades are B+ in every subject; except I got a B in algebra; I'm a darn good baseball player, and who knows where that will lead? I don't like arguing with you. But being a teenager today is a lot different than it was when you were my age."

Mother looked like she wanted to kill me. She glanced at Dad, her face clouded with anger. Mother turned her eyes on me, and the anger dissolved into sadness.

The Spencers, my mother's family, earned their nickname as "Stubborn Spencers," and Mother stood in the front row with that moniker. There were times when she personified stubborn, typifying her strict, sometimes harsh, upbringing. But she wasn't always that way. Mother played pranks on Dad and us sometimes. She appreciated good jokes, and laughed at herself on occasion. Like the time her newly-capped bottles of homemade tomato ketchup exploded one after the other. But those times didn't happen often enough.

CHAPTER 3

Shazam!

As I had feared, Prep's ace pitcher Sammy Williamson smoked us that Thursday. We didn't get a base hit off him until the sixth, and by that time the score was 6-0. I admit my head wasn't in the game. As we warmed up beforehand, I fielded one question after another about the murder, not only from my teammates, but also from a couple of the guys from Prep. No doubt about it, I played lousy. Sammy made me look like I didn't know which end of the bat was the handle. We were no longer in first place.

Mr. Angelone's obituary was in the paper. I don't usually read the obituaries, but his I did.

> *Erie Daily Times*, Friday, June 23, 1950: Benito "Benny" Angelone, suddenly, Monday, June 19, 1950. Mr. Angelone operated a barber shop at his residence. He is survived by his parents, Anthony M. Angelone and Rose Gusciora Angelone, Boston, Mass., a daughter, Mrs. Joseph Calaverri, Erie, Pa., two sons, Benito Angelone, Jr., Erie, Pa., and Joseph P. Angelone, Youngstown, Ohio. Other survivors include two sisters, Mrs. Rocco Mastandrea and Mrs. Michael DiStefano, Stoughton, Mass.,

a brother, Peter Angelone and three grand-children, all of Erie. Mr. Angelone was pre-ceded in death by his wife, the late Mary Romito Angelone. Requiem Mass will be celebrated in St. Patrick's Church, 127 Still-ings Street, South Boston, Monday, June 26, at 9:00 a.m. Interment will be in Calvary Cemetery, Helcher Street, South Boston."

I lowered the newspaper. I didn't know his first name was Benito, the same as Mussolini's. No wonder everybody called him Benny. He was fifty-six years old, which I think is kind of old. But Benny didn't act old. He could've rationed his intake of spaghetti and meatballs, but he was always humming a tune and telling funny jokes. His mother and Dad live in Boston. And Benny had a daughter and two sons, and three grandchildren. They must be feeling terrible. I mean, to have your father and grandfather die is bad, but to have him be shot and left out there in the weeds, is awful. I just hope they don't have to see him with that hole under his eye. I had a notion that Dolores and I should attend his funeral until I read that Mr. Angelone would be buried in a cemetery in South Bos-ton. Huh. I guess he was born and raised in Boston. Didn't know that, either. I got scissors and cut out his obituary to save the news about Benito Angelone.

That night, Dolores and I had to ride the bus uptown. We were just late enough to miss the begin-ning of the picture, so we had to sit through all the short subjects and the news about the Korean War to watch the opening scene. Dolores really got into the film, so she was not much interested in necking, even though we sat in the last row of the balcony.

During the bus ride home, Dolores was talking about the movie, and asking what I thought about this and that. She figured out that my mind was somewhere else, and it didn't sit well. Dolores scrunched over against the window. I apologized and explained what was bugging me.

"There's something nagging at me about the murder. It feels like I'm overlooking something important, but for the life of me I can't think what it is."

Dolores gave me a look. "Can't you leave that alone? Let the cops solve it."

"Look, honey," I said, taking her hand, "I wish we hadn't found Benny Angelone's body. But we did. And I wish I could stop thinking about it, but it won't go away. Stay with me, please."

"Oh, David." She squeezed my hand. "What am I going to do with you?" We got off the bus and walked across Lake Road. It was a wonderful summer night, and we were wasting it. I put my arms around her, pulled her close and kissed her. Man, Dolores knew how to kiss. A car approached and we stepped apart. Dolores noticed we were standing right in front of Angelone's Barber Shop. She giggled in that musical way she has. It was pretty hilarious in a weird way.

The Cooper's back yard included an outdoor chaise lounge situated under an elm. You couldn't see it from the house. Dolores had checked. A perfect place to end a summer night with one's girl. Just as we were about to lie down, I saw a cigarette glow. Someone was standing under the elm tree.

"Hello, kids. Did you enjoy the movie?"

"Yes, Daddy," answered Dolores.

"It was pretty good," I contributed.

"That's good." Mr. Cooper was not exactly the world's greatest conversationalist. He sure seemed to have an instinct for showing up at inconvenient times, though. "Nice night."

"Yes, sir, that's for sure."

He stubbed his cigarette against the tree and tossed it into a flower bed but made no move to go inside. It was no use. "Well," I said, "guess I'll get on home. Thanks, Dolores. I had a very nice time."

"Me, too, David." She would have said more, but Mr. Cooper put the kibosh on it.

"I'd appreciate it if you will secure the gate when you go into Chopka's. Sometimes his chicken gets in our yard and craps all over the place." *Don't let the gate hit you in the rear on your way out*, I thought. Actually, I didn't blame him for being protective. Dolores and her sister Judy were two snazzy-looking females, and he was going to make sure no one mistreated them in any way.

When I got home, Dad and Mother were at the dining room table playing 500 rummy and drinking beer with the Finsters. I cut a thick slice of homemade bread, slathered it with butter and peanut butter, and poured a big glass of milk. I took my plate up to my room to eat, regretting almost immediately that I hadn't fixed two slices. Jeannie's and Jimmy's bedroom doors were closed, but I saw a light shining from under Jeannie's door and heard music playing: Benny Goodman and his band doing "The King Porter Stomp". Jeannie could be a royal pain, but she had great taste in music. She was the only kid her age who dug Stan Kenton, which was pretty cool.

Benny Goodman's music got me thinking about the movie Dolores and I watched earlier, *Young Man With A Horn*. It's supposed to be about the great jazz trumpeter, Bix Beiderbecke. In the movie, Kirk Douglas plays Rick Martin. Rick has two drop-dead sexy women falling for him. He's a terrific musician with a top orchestra, but Rick Martin–that's Bix– makes some bad decisions. He acts big-in-the-head with his best friend who eventually gets smoked by a car, and Lauren Bacall, whose character is really weird, divorces him and he starts drinking like a fish, loses his job and his passion for music. His true love comes to the rescue, and they live happily until "The End" flashes on the screen. Did the real Bix Beiderbecke live happily the rest of his life, I wondered? Will my parents live happily for the rest of their lives? How about the Coopers? Sometimes I don't feel they're happy even now. Will I? Does anybody? I hoped so.

The peanut butter bread and the milk were gone, and I was thinking about going down to get me some more, but I didn't relish the idea of invading the card party. *Doggone that Mr. Cooper. I'd still be on that chaise lounge with Dolores if he hadn't been waiting.* It was too early to hit the hay, and the bookcase didn't hold any book I hadn't read. I turned on the little portable radio. *Let's see what the Pirates did tonight. Probably lost again.*

The local news broadcast led with the Angelone murder case. The police had pulled Mike Budzik in for questioning but refused to call him a suspect. They had no evidence against him. I had to agree. Just because I saw him in Angelone's two or three times proved nothing. Of course, he did kill that man in Cleveland for sixty dollars; so "Fat Stuff" could have shot Benny Angelone if Benny had crossed him on something. Did Mike Budzik remember me sitting there? I hoped to God not. I should've got my haircuts at Felton's Barber shop, even if Mr. Felton did charge more. I walked down the hall to the bathroom to take a leak. As I was drying my hands, I remembered the conversation between Mr. Angelone and that stocky guy behind the partly closed door Saturday. Officers Pelinski and Washington hadn't seemed interested in what I had heard, and they probably would have laughed their heads off about it if I had told them. What Benny said to him made no sense.

Last Saturday I rode my bike to Angelone's Barber Shop. The street door was open, so I walked in and took a seat. Benny was in the back room. The door wasn't shut tight, and I could hear Benny talking with someone. I didn't pay much attention at first. Like I said, this wasn't the first time I had to wait while Benny conducted business or whatever in his apartment. Dick Morrison, who lived across the street from Angelone's, told me his Dad said Benny Angelone was running numbers from his apartment. I had no clue what that meant, but I didn't want to seem stupid, so I just nodded.

The other guy sounded sore about something. I couldn't hear what they were saying until Mr. Angelone's squeaky voice got louder. He told this other person that he knew the names of all the characters in the Captain Marvel story, and insisted he be paid good money for the information. Angelone said something like, "I want the grand prize–$200,000." Now, at my age back then Captain Marvel was one of my favorite comic book characters. I remember thinking, "What contest?" I hadn't read of any contest.

The other guy seemed as flabbergasted as I was. "You what?" he asked, pretty loud. Then one of them pulled shut the door and that's all I heard. A few minutes later the back room door swung open, and this tough-looking stocky guy stood in the doorway, surprised as all get-out to see me sitting there. He looked like he wanted to say something to me, but he just turned and said, "Hey, Benny, you got a customer." He walked back into the room and closed the door. I couldn't make out what he said to Benny, but in a matter of seconds he came out, our eyes met for a second before he went out onto the sidewalk, strode past the window, and was gone.

Mr. Angelone came into the shop, whistling between his teeth, wrapped a strip of tissue paper around my neck, and fastened the cloth over the front of me. "So, Bucko," he opened, "same as usual?"

"Yeah, that'll be good," I answered. He picked

up a comb and parted my hair.

"How long you been waiting in here?"

"Not long. A minute, maybe."

"That's good. I don't want to keep one of my regular customers waiting." And that was that.

I took off my shoes and laid across the bed. I remember asking myself if I should tell Pelinski and Washington what I'd overheard. What, that Benny Angelone knew the names of characters in a Captain Marvel comic book story? Even as a 17-year-old I knew they'd see this as a big nothing. Lying across my bed that night, half-listening to the ball game I let my imagination loose. Maybe the stocky guy murdered Mr. Angelone because there really was a prize for knowing all the good and bad characters, and he wanted the prize money for himself.

God, what a loamy imagination I had in those days. I got up off the bed, put on my pjs, and switched off the light. Those two detectives would have laughed their heads off.

CHAPTER 4

A Door Closes, Another Opens

The next morning Dad and Mother had scheduled one of their infrequent but annoying family conferences. I knew it as soon as I got to the bathroom at the top of the stairs. I smelled pancakes cooking, which was solid evidence of an impending meeting. Mother never cooked pancakes for breakfast except when she and Dad wanted to tell us kids something they felt strongly about. She made pancakes for Saturday suppers lots of times, but never for breakfast.

As I took a leak and scrubbed my teeth, I wondered what would be on the agenda. Since they hadn't announced it ahead of time, Jimmy, Jeannie, and I would have no opportunity to present our ideas, issues, or gripes on the chosen subject. No, Mother and Dad would control the agenda. Jeannie was waiting in the hall.

"Do you smell pancakes?" Not waiting for an answer, she continued, "what did you do now?"

"They discovered my plan for killing you in your sleep with my old Boy Scout hatchet, Pimples." "Mother!" Jeannie yelled. "David called me Pimples."

Dad's voice rolled up the steps. "That's enough, you two. Now get dressed and get down here. Your mother and I want to talk to you. Your brother's been here for fifteen minutes already."

I have to admit, serving us pancakes for these family meetings was a stroke of genius. Mother made her pancakes from scratch with flour, eggs, and fresh buttermilk. No "Pancakes in a Box" for her. Mother greased the cast iron skillet with a bacon rind, testing the temperature by sprinkling a few drops of water onto the griddle's surface. When the water rolled and skidded like balls of mercury, she plopped down four hefty dollops of batter and watched until the bubbles burst before flipping the cakes. Oh, could she make pancakes.

My standard pancake-eating method was to alternate soaking the first plate of cakes in real maple syrup and the next in Mother's home-made crabapple jelly. The sausage from Bender's Meats in the 12th Street Market was the best ever. It cut the sweetness of the butter and maple syrup.

When we'd finished all the pancakes and the sausage was nothing but a lingering hint on the tongue of sage and pork, Dad opened the meeting. "Your mother and I have some news to share," he began, a funny kind of smile on his face. Jeannie and I shot each other a quizzical look. "Mr. Garland, my boss at Hickman, told me on Wednesday he's pleased with my work, so pleased that he's offered me the position of Sales Manager for western Pennsylvania and parts of Ohio and West Virginia, beginning in September. That means I'll have an office at the main office, so we'll be living in Pittsburgh."

Mother chimed in merrily. "As you kids know, we've been renting this house since we moved here eleven years ago. But with your Dad's new position, we'll be able to buy our own home."

"And" Dad added, "we'll be able to have a car of our own."

Whoopie ding dong, I thought. *There goes my senior year shot to blazes, not to mention my relationship with Dolores.* The only thing I remembered about Pittsburgh was the smoke and grit. Sometimes the smoke from the steel and coke plants turned the sky nearly as black as midnight. We'd get to see our relatives more often, which at my age was a positive. I had lots of fun with my cousins. And of course, my favorite Major League team was the Pirates, even though they weren't playing too hot lately.

"Will we get to ride a streetcar to school?" asked Jimmy. *What a stupe. Was that all he could think of?* Hearing a negative answer, he lost interest. Jeannie just sat there. She would have started eighth grade at East High after Labor Day. She still hated boys; at least she still hated me, but she would have to part from her best friend, Sally.

"Well," Dad asked, "what do you think?"

"David," Mother cut in before any of us could say anything, "we realize how hard this will be for you, being your senior year and all. But you'll make new friends. You're outgoing and smart, and the schoolwork won't be any more difficult." She didn't mention Dolores. Getting me away from Dolores must have been a big plus in this for her.

"I have no idea where we'll be living, but of course your mother and I want you three to have the benefit of good schools," Dad put in, his tone much too cheerful. "Your uncle Art told me the Pittsburgh area schools have terrific baseball programs." A bone. Dad had thrown a bone my way. Big deal.

"So, Jeannie, what do you have to say?" Maybe Jeannie would have something enthusiastic to say. They knew they weren't going to hear anything positive from me. Hey, don't get me wrong. Dad worked his tail off for Hickman, and he was an excellent salesman, probably Hickman's best. I used to go with him on one or two trips every summer. On one of those trips to Dunkirk, New York I ate my first cheeseburger and drank my first chocolate milkshake. Everyone liked Dad, even the secretaries; maybe especially the secretaries, because Dad knew their first names, and always asked about their husbands and kids. He deserved the promotion, and I knew he'd do a terrific job.

But I didn't say any of this to him, a fact of which I'm not proud. Instead I sulked like a little kid who can't have any more ice cream. All I was thinking was what would life be like without Dolores? It wasn't fair to expect me to give up both my senior year at East and Dolores, too. Cheap trick to cook pancakes for this catastrophe.

"What about you, Davey?" Mother reverted to her pet name she gave me when I was in kindergarten. "Your father and I want to hear what you think."

"Whatever," I grunted, pushing back the chair. The screen door slammed shut on its spring. So this is how my world ends.

I started walking down Euclid toward

the lake. Jim Hudak and his brother, Rich, were playing catch on the street. "Hey, Dave, go get your glove.
There's some guys getting up a ball game behind Edi-
son." A ball game. My life was ending in September
and these dumb squirts wanted me to play baseball.

At the corner of Second Street I saw
Mr. Weinbrenner carrying a stupid piece of wood he
had scrounged from the lake. He had retired from GE
right after the war, and now he spent part of every
cotton-pickin' day walking the narrow beaches looking for driftwood and other crap to make into dumb-
looking stuff. Mr. Weinbrenner smiled and said hello.
He looked like he was ready to go into a long conversation, so I just mumbled, "Good morning," without
even looking at his face and kept moving on. If I live to
be as ancient as Mr. Weinbrenner, I hope I don't spend
my days doing goofy stuff.

There was an offshore breeze, so Lake Erie
was pretty smooth. You could smell the chemicals the
paper company discharged into the water from the
plant about a mile to the west. The water was foamy
gray for about a half mile out from shore. All the parents in the neighborhood outlawed swimming there.
They threatened dire punishment and brought up the
specter of infantile paralysis. They could have saved
their breath. No kid in his or her right mind would
even dip a bare foot in that chemical stew.

I walked east along the top of the cliff toward
Four Mile Creek. During the war, George, Johnny, Bill,
sometimes Bobby, and I would play war here. It was all
the more realistic when GE was test-firing .50 caliber

machine guns with live tracer ammunition out over the water. I found a place in the grass where I could dangle my legs over the edge of the shale cliffs.

There was a guy fishing from a small boat out beyond the gray water. He was drift fishing, probably for yellow pike. Some call them walleyes. I used to fish sometimes with Dad and Uncle Bob, mostly over in Misery Bay on the peninsula. They'd rent a rowboat at the lagoons, and one of them would row out to the bay. Even though I was just a little kid, Uncle Bob insisted that I would have the honor of putting the anchor overboard. First time I did it I tossed the darn thing, and the splash thoroughly wet Uncle Bob and drowned out his pipe. He didn't get mad, though. He just showed me how to do it without scaring away every fish in the lake.

Dad liked to fish, but two things happened that put a damper on our fishing excursions. When I was in fifth–no, fourth grade, a friend of mine, Will Peterson, went out fishing with his Dad. They went fishing in Mr. Peterson's boat on Presque Isle Bay. It was evening and some drunken fool in a speedboat going about ninety cut their boat in half and killed them both. Going fishing in a boat scared me for a long while. Once I got over the heebie-jeebies about the Peterson tragedy, Dad's work had become so demanding he didn't have much time to have fun.

I caught a grasshopper and made him spit in my hand. It looked just like tobacco juice. I opened my hand, and it flew off, wings clattering, making an arcing turn away from the cliff. What was I doing?

Sitting there pouting like a little twerp. Thinking the world revolved around me. It was not one of my best moments. I knew Dad deserved the promotion. There was no question of that. And yet, all I thought about that morning was why did it have to happen to me right now? I would have to begin my senior year in a new school. I wouldn't know anyone. I'd been class-mates with some of my East High friends since first grade.

I was consumed with the idea of losing Do-lores. I knew that morning someone would make a move on her. There wasn't a snowball's chance we would still go steady from a distance. I didn't think of the stress Dad might feel in a management position, with new and unanticipated responsibilities, prob-ably working with at least some people he did not know, or with whom he had never worked with. I had no thought for mother's work to get all our household goods and clothing packed, hire a moving company, check out schools in Pittsburgh, and look for a suit-able home for us. Nor did I spend any thoughts for my brother and sister. It would be a difficult adjustment for Jeannie. But it was all about me as I sat on the cliff top that morning. It can be painful and humiliating to see yourself from the perspective of a few years.

Then suddenly I was crying. I had myself a huge self-pity party that day. At last I stood. I looked out at the lake. The guy in the boat had floated out of sight.

I dragged on home. As I walked down the driveway, I remembered I was supposed to cut Dr.

Lawson's grass that day. I wasn't in the mood to do that job any time, but not that afternoon, especially. His yard was at least two miles across. He had one of those new gas-powered rotary mowers, but he wouldn't let me use it. So, every other Saturday I pulled our hand-powered push mower over there behind my bike. He paid me five bucks, which was more than Bobby Carney got for doing Brebners' yard, and Bobby had to hand-trim around trees and shrubs

Dad's car wasn't in the driveway, but Mother was waiting for me. She was not pleased with my reaction to Dad's promotion announcement, and she let me know in no uncertain terms.

"I didn't raise you to be selfish and rude to your parents, mister. I can see right through you. All you care about is that Cooper girl. You had no business stomping out of the house like some little baby who didn't get his way. You hurt your father's feelings very badly."

What could I say? Mother was right. I said I was very sorry and tried to explain, but she kept at it and after a couple more minutes of it I just wanted to get out of there. Sometimes Mother went through several red lights after making her point. "And what's more, mister, you are not allowed to see Dolores for a week, do you hear me?"

That was a cheap shot, in my estimation. But if I protested, the jail sentence would expand to two weeks, so I kept my mouth closed. Sometimes I hated my mother. But at that particular moment that day I hated myself.

"Do you hear me?"

"Yes."

"Yes, what?" She was pushing me, maybe hoping I'd blow my stack. "Yes, Mother." She began to run out of steam, and my mind was thinking of ways I could sneak over to see Dolores. It's human nature. If someone tells you not to do something, chances are you're gonna go right out and do it. Finding a way to be with Dolores this week had become my mission in life.

"Aren't you supposed to mow Dr. Lawson's grass today?" Boy, Mother had a mind like a steel trap. She never wrote notes to herself but kept all our schedules and daily chores in her head.

"Yes. I'll get over there, soon as I eat lunch."

The phone rang and she went into Dad's office to answer it. I grabbed some slices of ring baloney from the fridge, cut a thick slice of bread, coated it with butter and mustard, and ducked out the back door. I swung open the left-side garage door with one hand, jamming the baloney sandwich into my mouth with the other. I wanted to get the heck out of the driveway before Mother finished the phone call. The old reel mower hummed along behind the bike as I coasted down the hill and rolled left on Second Street for a block, then right on Sanford. Most of the houses in our neighborhood were two-story frame or brick, constructed in the 1930s or 40s. As I think about it, there was only one up-and-down duplex. Lakeside Drive which paralleled the lake shore had some expensive homes, but the three blocks from there to

East Lake Road were all nice but modest homes. All but two homes in those blocks had small strips of front lawn and large backyards. Only the Nortons and the Lawsons had front grass areas that required more than five passes with a mower. A few had side yards big enough to throw a football, play croquet, or horseshoes, and there were a couple of vacant corner lots for baseball and football.

At the Lawson's house, I surprised Cynthia Lawson who was sunbathing on a beach towel in her backyard. Cynthia was a sophomore in college somewhere in Michigan. She had these dark eyes and long lashes, and the rest of her wasn't hard to look at either, especially in a bathing suit. "Hi, Cynthia," I said, pushing the mower ahead of me. Cynthia lifted herself onto one elbow and flicked her sunglasses down her nose so she could give me the once-over.

"David, how nice to see you. I suppose I'll have to move, won't I?"

"Yeah, unless you want me to do the front yard first." Cynthia had changed since the previous summer, and for the better, in my estimation.

She stood, picking up her towel and came over to me. I was still hanging onto the mower handle like some moron. "I saw your picture in the paper. Did you really see the man who was murdered down behind Sonnhalter's?"

"Yeah."

"You must be really brave," she murmured, her eyes never moving from my face. Had the news article mentioned I had puked? I hoped not.

"Not really," I said, finally releasing the mower. Cynthia was scaring me just about as much as Benny's body had.

"What did he look like?" Her long black hair shone like a crow's feathers.

"Who? Mr. Angelone?" She nodded, still looking at me like I was a T-bone steak. "Well, he was just laying there."

"Lying there," Cynthia corrected me.

"He was lying there in the grass on his back with his eyes open, but that's all I can tell you, 'cause the police want to keep the details secret." She was impressed.

"What were you doing on that lane back of Sonnhalter's? Were you by yourself?" she smiled in a foxy way, "or making out with Dolores? Are you and she still going steady, David, or have you moved on to new adventures?" Cynthia's eyes were still fixed on me. Holy smoke, didn't she ever blink?

"Well, yeah, Dolores and I are steady."

"So you were at Sonnhalter's with Dolores. She's a lucky girl." My throat felt like I had swallowed a chicken bone.

"Thanks," I managed to croak. "Hey, I better get this grass cut." Cynthia put her hand on my arm.

"I made some lemonade. When you get hot, come on in and I'll give you some. My parents aren't home." She let her hand slide down my arm before letting go and walked into the house. *When* I get hot? I **was** hot. I hung my tee shirt on one of the lounge chairs and got to work. Soon the sweat was dripping off my chin. The Lawson yard didn't have any trees, so there was no shade.

I took a break under the roof of the back patio, wiping myself with my shirt. Suddenly something icy cold touched my back. I jumped about a foot. Cynthia laughed. She handed me a tall glass of lemonade. "Come in where it's cool. The air conditioning's on." She didn't have to invite me twice.

We went into the living room and Cynthia lowered herself onto a leather sofa. "You work fast, David." *Not as fast as you*, I thought. "Here, sit beside me." I took a swig of the lemonade.

"I better get back to the grass," I said without conviction.

"There's plenty of time for that," reasoned Cynthia. The cool air felt terrific, and she looked terrific.

"Let me get my shirt," I said. "I don't want to get sweat on your couch."

"It's leather, David. Liquid wipes right off." What the heck. I sat on the edge of the cushion. Boy oh boy, did Cynthia smell wonderful. I couldn't help myself.

"You smell terrific," I said, immediately wishing I hadn't.

"Really? You like it?"

"Uh-huh . . . I mean, yeah, I do."

"The perfume is called Wood Hue," Cynthia said. The way she pronounced it sounded like 'Would you?'

"That's nice," I said, debonair as a hunk of

wilted lettuce. My sense of smell must have been blocking my brain from intelligent conversation. Or maybe it was Cynthia, who, to my complete surprise, had slid along the leather until she was practically sitting on my lap.

"You've really changed since I saw you last summer, David. You've filled out and grown taller." Surreptitiously I tightened the muscles in my right arm, just in case Cynthia might decide to check me out.

"You think so?" I said. "Thanks, Cynthia." I was having difficulty breathing normally. My arm started to ache from holding it tight as a stone.

"What about me, David?" She had her eyes locked on mine again. "Have I changed any since last summer?" I needed to get outside.

"You have," I said.

"And do you like the changes?"

"Very much. You're... really..." Whoa! How did my hand get on her leg? Cynthia twisted around and kissed me. Now I thought . . .uh, . . . Dolores . . . really knew how to kiss. But she was an apprentice compared to Cynthia Lawson. While she French-kissed me she unbuckled my belt and slid down the fly zipper. I couldn't believe this was happening so naturally, so easily. I never imagined a beautiful college girl would want to have sex with me. Cynthia had no inhibitions, and she led me to that same mountain top, and I never wanted to leave. At the last second, she whispered, "Not inside me."

Afterward we were laying–lying–on the slippery leather, her mouth and tongue playing on my ear. Cynthia asked, "How often do you mow our lawn?"

"Once every other week, but if you take the hose and water it real good every morning, it'll need to be mowed once a week at least." Cynthia cracked up laughing and started kissing me again. I couldn't believe what had happened, and how much I wanted it to happen again.

I finally finished the grass and was actually thinking about going back in to Cynthia, when Dr. Lawson pulled up the drive.

"Glad I caught you, David," he said. For a split second I thought he knew about Cynthia and me! "Come on in for a minute, and I'll pay you." I was hoping to catch sight of Cynthia, but she was somewhere else, probably in her bedroom. He handed me a $5 bill. "You did a good job. The lawn looks great."

"Thank you, Dr. Lawson." I had my hand on the screen door handle and was about to go when I said, "You know, the grass seemed pretty high today. "Do you think I should cut it more often, say, once a week?"

"I'll let you be the judge, David. If you think you need to come once a week, that's okay with me."

Pumping my bike hard up Sanford, one hand towing the mower behind, I kept remembering and feeling the sensations of making it with Cynthia. Then I would think of Dolores and how we had taken it for granted that we would do it together for the first time. What a rat I am. How could I have been unfaithful to Dolores? And then I would see Cynthia and feel her skin against mine. I was a mess. Would I have allowed this to happen if we weren't moving to Pittsburgh in a couple of months? Yeah, I would have.

The first thing I did after stowing my bike and the mower in the garage was to apologize to Dad for being a world-class jerk. I told him I was proud, and happy for him, that he deserved the promotion.

"Dad, I'm so ashamed of myself. Please forgive me. I love you."

He was great. He hugged me and told me he forgave me. Dad thanked me for apologizing and said he understood why I reacted that way.

Although I believed Dad forgave me, I wasn't able to forgive myself. In fact, I was taken aback at what I had done. I worshipped my Dad, and I knew my behavior had cut him deeply. And why? Because I loved Dolores. Yeah, I loved her so much I had sex with Cynthia two hours after hurting my Dad. What really shook me was how quickly and completely I had forgotten Dolores. The truth hit me: I hadn't considered the feelings of anybody but my own that day.

Dad hugged me again. I felt tears brimming. We stepped apart. His eyes were wet. "You OK, Dave?" I nodded. "Yeah, OK." I opened the door. He patted my shoulder.

"I'd appreciate if you wouldn't tell anyone about our move just yet. Your mother and I have a lot of loose ends to tie in the next few days. The fewer people who know of this the smoother it will be. Jeannie and Jimmy got the same message."

"OK, Dad. Will do."

Mother was alone, peeling potatoes in the kitchen. She seemed to have calmed down somewhat, so I apologized to her again, since she hadn't let me do it earlier. "Don't you ever act that way again, David Elliott," she said, pointing the potato peeler at me. What a relief. She had forgiven me. But as far as lifting the ban on seeing Dolores, no dice. Considering my afternoon escapade with Cynthia Lawson, I wasn't looking forward to spending time with Dolores in the immediate future anyways. I had decided to break the news about our move to her face-to-face. The intervening period of silence and separation would give me time to decide the best approach.

After supper, I phoned Dolores to tell her I was in the dog house, and my punishment was a week without her.

"For heaven's sake, David, what on earth did you do?"

"Well, we had a family . . . Uh, that is, I got mad about something and shot off my mouth to Dad and Mother. this morning."

"It was about me, wasn't it?"

"It's a family matter and I'm going to keep it inside the family."

"You're not going to tell me?"

"That's right."

"Why not? Don't you trust me?"

"Trust has nothing to do with this. The only thing you need to know is that I screwed up, and I'm grounded. Truthfully, I deserved my punishment."

"I don't appreciate being treated like a . . . like a

stranger. I thought we agreed to tell each other everything. You hurt me."

"Come on, Dolores, you're . . ."

"Daddy said he may take Monday off so we can have the whole weekend to spend Fourth of July with my Aunt Barbara's family at their cottage on Chautauqua Lake. When I find out for sure, I'll let you know, unlike you." The line went dead.

There was a knot in my stomach. A future—even the immediate future with Dolores—looked dark.

CHAPTER 5

News From Coudersport

Next morning we went to church as we did most Sundays. My best friend, Jim Shea, and his parents sat right behind us. Jim and I had been friends ever since 5th grade when during Vacation Bible School we glued Sister Beverly to her chair. She wasn't a real church sister or anything. We just called her that in private because she always gave the impression that she was one of Jesus's best friends. Neither of us figured she would lose her balance when she tried to stand, but she did. She wasn't hurt or anything, but someone squealed on us, and we really caught hell from our parents. Jim's mother punished him by making him stay home from the rest of Vacation Bible School. Some punishment. It seemed like a reward to me, and I told Jim so. My mother not only made me apologize to Sister Beverly and go to Vacation Bible School every morning, but also made me wash our windows for a whole year.

Jim and I played ball for Sementelli's Pizza in the Times League during our Junior High days. I think that's when we started calling each other by our last names. Now he pitched for Erie Academy, and we would be playing them Tuesday. As soon as the organist started in on the postlude, which to us was basically a musical dismissal bell, Shea smacked me in the arm.

"Hey, Ellie, guess who's pitching against you bums Tuesday?"

"What?" I said, "Academy doesn't have any good pitchers left?" Shea was tough to hit. His best pitch was a wicked curve, but his fast ball had some zip to it. *Shoot*, I said to myself. *We faced Sammy Williamson last game, now Jim Shea. Beating him and his team would be difficult.* When our families were out of earshot, Shea asked about Benny Angelone's murder.

"I've never seen a dead person," Shea said, except in a funeral home. How come you were by the lake?" Then he answered his own question. "Oh, yeah. Dolores. Right?"

"Right."

"I read *I, the Jury* by Mickey Spillane, and he wrote that this dead woman had her eyes open. Were Benny's eyes open?"

"Yeah. Look, Shea, I'm not allowed to talk about it." He ignored me.

"Who do you think killed him? I bet it was somebody connected to the numbers racket."

"Numbers racket? Where'd you get that?"

"It was in the paper that your barber was running a numbers joint. Don't you read the paper, Ellie?"

"Sure. Heck-sakes, Mr. Angelone's been cutting my hair for two years. Don't you think I know he was in the numbers game?" Jim Shea pressed his theory as we walked along West 10th to where the family cars were parked.

"I figure Benny was cheating Mike Budzik out of a bunch of money and Budzik caught on and wiped him out," he said, poking my chest. "Wanna bet me?" "I'd rather bet we beat you Tuesday. That's a sure thing, pal." He laughed and said he didn't want to take my money. "Jim," Mr. Shea called, "Come on. Your grandmother's waiting on us for dinner."

At our home, Sunday dinner after church always was a white linen tablecloth, best-china and silverware affair. Mother was a terrific cook and pie baker, and today she was going all out: prime rib roast beef, mashed potatoes, and green beans from Dad's garden. She had baked a sour cherry pie, one of my favorite kinds. Maybe she was trying to make us kids feel better about moving. Jeannie was helping in the kitchen and Jimmy was lying on the floor in Dad's office, playing war with his lead soldiers or something. Dad and I were sitting in the living room reading the Sunday paper. He had grabbed the Sports section, so I waded into the news while waiting for him to finish reading about the woebegone Pittsburgh Pirates.

I flicked a couple of pages past reports of the intensifying war in Korea and the politics in Washington to news from the state. Geez, some Amish boy from Lebanon got stomped to death by a bull. He was only ten and jumped into the bull's pen to retrieve his hat. What a horrible way to die. From what I read, the kid's father refused to do anything to the bull, saying the animal had acted on instinct. Amish folks are very forgiving people.

When "Fat Stuff" Budzik kicked that guy to death in Cleveland, he hadn't acted on instinct. He was sending a message out there that he was no one to mess with. He did it deliberately. Yet, like the bull, he wasn't punished. Maybe Shea's idea that Budzik shot Mr. Angelone wasn't that far-fetched after all.

Down at the bottom of the page was a story about a robbery in Coudersport. "Hey, Dad, doesn't Mother's cousin Mabel work in some store in Coudersport?"

"Uh-huh." Turns out the Pirates had beat the Cards, and he was really absorbed in the re-cap.

"What's the name of the store?"

"I don't know, Dave. Ask your mother."

"Was it Rosenbloom's?"

"What?"

"The name of the store where Mabel works. Was it Rosenbloom's Men's and Boy's Store?"

Dad lowered the paper. "Can't you see I'm reading? I said ask your mother. It's her cousin."

Dinner preparations were nearing the finish line. The roast beef was relaxing on the sideboard. Jeannie was slopping butter on the peas. Mother was whipping the potatoes into shape.

"Mother, your cousin Mabel from Coudersport–what's the name of the store where she works?"

"Rosenbloom's," she said without missing a beat on the potato masher.

"Well, she may have some exciting news to

tell in her next letter. Two crooks from Boston broke in and robbed the store last week." That got her attention.

"Mabel's store? Where on earth did you learn that?"

"It's in the paper. Special to the Erie papers from the Coudersport Endeavor, on page seven. These two guys, Stanley Gusciora and Joseph O'Keefe, were arrested for going through a stop light in Towanda, and the cops found guns, plus sports coats and stuff marked with the Rosenbloom label in their car."

Mother put the pot of potatoes back on the stove and wiped her hands on her apron. "For goodness' sake. Let me see." She read the brief item and handed me the paper while she resumed whipping the potatoes. "Thank goodness no one was hurt. They had guns. What if they had robbed the store when it was open? Harold," she called, "will you carve the roast?"

While Dad sharpened the carving knife, Mother filled him in. Dad said they must be amateur crooks to run a traffic light with stolen property in plain sight in the back seat. Mother said she wanted to call Mabel right after dinner.

"Em, a long distance call during the day? If you want to talk with Mabel, call her after eleven o'clock tonight when the rates are lower."

"It's Sunday, Harold," she said. "Long distance rates are already low on weekends. I want to hear what Mabel has to say. You know her; she'll know the whole story."

"Yes," said Dad, "and what she doesn't know

she'll make up." Mother laughed in agreement.

As it turned out, Mabel didn't know much about the robbery other than what she had read in the paper. She had been too busy to write Mother, she told her, because the employees had to take inventory of the clothing so the insurance company could figure out how much to reimburse Rosenbloom's.

Pretty soon Mother and Mabel shifted the conversation to family matters, and I reread the article from Coudersport. It struck me as odd that two guys from Boston had robbed a gun store in Kane, Pennsylvania and a clothing store in Coudersport. Then they got arrested in Towanda. Which meant they were traveling east along Route 6. They would get to Kane first, then Coudersport, then Towanda. I guessed they were heading back to Boston from somewhere and decided they'd have easy pickings in these sleepy little towns. Still, Kane was a long way from Boston, even if my guess about the easy pickings was correct. What, there aren't gun stores and clothing stores in Boston to rob?

An event that seems to have no connection to you sometimes changes things in a really big way, and you never see it coming, and that's a good thing. If you could see into the future, what's out there might scare you to death.

CHAPTER 6

The Thrill of Victory and the Agony of Plans Thwarted

Coach Gil didn't call practice that Monday, even though we had a game with Academy on Tuesday, a game we had to win if we were going to have a shot at making the playoffs next month. Bobby Russell, the team captain, phoned to say he and a couple other guys were going to meet at our practice field next to the Uniflow Corporation plant Monday evening to do some batting and fielding.

Bobby had graduated in May, and he took his leadership seriously. This was his final season playing for East High. I draped my spikes and glove over the handlebars and rode my bike to Uniflow, which was about a mile from the house. As I pedaled along past Hammermill Paper Company and the cemetery, I thought about moving to Pittsburgh. It wouldn't be easy leaving my buddies. I enjoyed my classes at East, too. There were some fine teachers on the faculty, especially Miss Bryant and Mr. Harbison.

As it turned out, most of the team showed up and we had a pretty good practice, even if we were short on bats and balls. Toward the end of practice, I saw Dad standing behind the backstop. He had played semi-pro baseball in Pittsburgh when he was young, and his brother Art said Dad would have been a professional baseball player, maybe even in the majors, if he hadn't injured his leg.

After the other guys left, Dad walked onto the field near home plate, carrying an old duffel bag bulging with baseballs. He and I agreed that Jim would throw plenty of curveballs in tomorrow's game. I had been having difficulty hitting curves lately. Dad suggested I move up to the front of the batter's box, which would give me a chance to hit the pitch before it broke.

Then Dad asked for my glove and went out to the mound and threw me one curveball after another until I swear his arm must have been ready to fall off. But man, it really helped. I was blistering those pitches. I hoped it would carry over to the game. Although I realized Dad was not the pitcher Shea was.

The Academy game was the first game of a doubleheader. Shea was as hot as the weather. But so was Lukey Lukasheski, our big right-hander. Neither team could find a way to score until the top of the ninth when Academy pushed across two runs. I knew Shea could just about taste victory. He had this "you ain't gotta chance" look in his eyes as he finished his warm-ups. After he struck out Lukey and Dickie grounded out, our chances looked bleak. But Bobby Russell singled, and Mel doubled. Two out, two on, and I stepped into the batter's box. Cabeloff ran like a scalded cat, so a single from me could tie the score.

Before he threw the first pitch, Shea grinned a big grin at me, and I grinned right back. We were telling each other this was fun, no matter what happened.

He knew I didn't often swing at the first pitch, so he fired a fastball for a strike. Then a curveball, which the umpire said was a strike. To this day I still think it was low for what should have been ball one. Now Shea had me in a hole. I watched him shake off his catcher, and somehow I knew what was coming next. A curve. Shea's best pitch. He went into his stretch. The curve ball just started to drop when I got hold of it. I hit it on top of the school roof in right field. Game over. As I ran across home plate, I looked at Dad in the stands and we were laughing and crying.

Shea was the first to shake my hand.

The next morning, *The Erie Times* had a swell picture of me crossing home plate with the winning run, and the headline on the Sports Page read ELLIOTT LEADS WARRIORS: HOMERS TO BEAT ACADEMY, 3-2.

Thursday we had a big game against Prep. It was big 'cause we had to win to get into the playoffs. Baseball's a funny game. Prep had shellacked us two games in a row. But that Thursday, we cleaned their clocks. We had six runs before they came to bat, and we enjoyed every minute of white washing them, 7-0. East High was in the high school baseball championship playoffs!

Saturday my exile from Dolores was up, so I phoned her, but there was no answer. I figured she was at her aunt's cottage on Chautauqua Lake. Maybe it was for the best.

It hadn't rained since the previous Saturday, but maybe Cynthia had been watering the grass at her house, so I saddled up and pulled the mower to Lawsons. Who knows? If she hadn't goosed the grass along, then maybe I wouldn't have to cut the grass at all which would give us more time together.

I rolled to the back of the drive. Cynthia was laying–lying –on a chaise lounge, her bathing suit showing her off to perfection.

She had heard the whir of the reel and stood, smiling. "David!" she said in a loud voice. "Are you here to mow?" Still louder. Before I could reply, the back door opened, and out walked Dr. Lawson.

"Ah, Dave, I should have phoned. I'm not on call at the hospital this weekend, so I'll take your spot behind the mower this afternoon." I snuck a glance at Cynthia, whose facial expression communicated her disappointment.

"I'm surprised how much the grass grew this week, seeing as how we didn't get any rain," he observed. "Wish a happy Fourth to your parents. By the way," Dr. Lawson clapped me on the shoulder, "Congratulations on winning the game the other night. Great picture of you scoring after your four-bagger."

"Thank you, sir," I responded. After another sidelong glance at the lovely Cynthia, I prepared to leave.

"See you next Saturday, David," Cynthia called.

"Sure thing," I said. Grabbing the mower handle, I swung my right leg over the crossbar, lost my balance, and just about crushed my nuts on the metal. It just about made me faint.

CHAPTER 7

Cousin Judy Makes an Observation
and Dolores Makes an Offer

Monday afternoon, July 3, Dad's younger brother Art and his family drove up from Pittsburgh to spend the Fourth with us. Aunt Rosalie and our cousins, Judy and JoAnn, brought lots of picnic food. Dad had a case of Koehler's beer, and plenty of root beer for us kids. Judy was my age. JoAnn and Jeannie had been born just two months apart, so we all got along great.

JoAnn, Jeannie, and Jimmy broke out the Monopoly game and were spread out on the floor of the front porch. Judy hugged me and told me she was happy that we were moving, which meant we would see each other more often, but she sympathized with me about my senior year, and the likely end of my relationship with Dolores. Judy and her boyfriend had recently called it quits, so she knew how low I was feeling.

Judy proposed the two of us go for a walk to the lake. The adults were sitting under the big maple in the backyard, smoking, armed with cold beers, catching up on family stuff, so they were okay with it. Although Mother looked like she wanted to nix the idea, probably because she intuited I'd show Judy the murder scene, but she just said, "We'll be eating in about an hour, so don't be too long."

Judy had heard all about Benny Angelone. As soon as we got to the street, she insisted on seeing where I had found his body along with all the details.

When we arrived at the site, things had changed. The entrance to the dirt road was chained off. A "No Trespassing" sign hung from the chain. Judy and I skirted the barrier and made our way to the spot where Benny Angelone's body had lain. The vines and weeds were completely trampled, and most of the small trees and shrubs showed broken branches.

"What's the matter?" Judy asked when I grabbed her arm.

"Someone's been here. Looks like he wanted to find something. The body was lying over there, hidden behind weeds and honeysuckle vines. Now they're torn up."

"Who was here? The killer?"

"Maybe," I said.

"What the heck could he have been looking for? Something that would pin the murder on him." Judy answered her own question.

"Good thought, cuz. If you're right, then the next question is, did he find whatever it was?"

"Judging from the way this whole area is ripped and trampled, my guess is he didn't find it, or else he didn't find it until he had gone over the whole area," she declared.

"We can't know if he found anything or not. In fact, we have no way to know if the killer or the cops trampled this area."

"Or it might have been curiosity seekers. There

was a sensational double murder in New Jersey I think, where a throng of neighbors and other on-lookers overran the crime scene before the police arrived. They picked up cartridge shells, handed around the note left by the murderer. They totally comprom-ised - I think that's the right term - the area. The cops never have caught the killer."

"When did that happen?"

"Umm, I'm pretty sure it was 1922. I read about it in True Crime magazine. I have a subscription."

I looked at her. I couldn't have been more surprised if Judy had told me she was a secret agent of the CIA. "You . . . read . . . True Crime?"

She shrugged. "Sure. So, this is where you and – it's Dolores isn't it – made out?"

"Almost. Finding a dead body changed things."

Judy chuckled. "I bet it did." How did she react to the news of your move?"

"She doesn't know yet. Dad asked us to keep mum until he and Mother took care of some things."

Judy glanced at her wristwatch. "We'd better start back. We've been gone almost an hour." Reluc-tantly, I agreed. "By the way," she added, "did you no-tice the dried vomit?" Sometimes my cousin was too observant.

When we got back home, Dad was cook-ing hot dogs and hamburgers on the charcoal grill, a bottle of beer in one hand, tongs in the other. Uncle Art was telling him something hilarious judging from their laughter. Jimmy rushed up to announce he had won the Monopoly game, which he didn't have to do. The disgust on JoAnn and Jeannie's faces told the story. One day, he'd need to learn how to be a good winner.

July Fourth brought with it a light but steady rain, and Dad and Uncle Art talked about going to a movie instead of going to the Peninsula for a picnic and swimming. Judy and JoAnn looked as gloomy as the cloudy sky. After all, Jimmy, Jeannie, and I could swim and ride waves in Lake Erie often, but they had to swim in a pool with about a thousand other people. They had been eager to dive into the waves and feel the cool, ripple-y sand of the lake bottom underfoot. We pleaded, and Jimmy was on the verge of launching a four-star tantrum.

JoAnn saved the day, making the point that we'd get wet swimming anyway. Everyone laughed, and we packed the cars and left for the peninsula. What with the polio scare and the crumby bath houses on Presque Isle, we always put on our bathing suits at home. Afterwards we took turns toweling off and dressing in the car, windows draped with beach towels. I rode with Judy in the back seat of Uncle Art's big new Buick; JoAnn rode in our car with Jeannie and Jimmy.

Aunt Rosalie kept up a steady flow of talk aimed at my uncle in her raspy cigarette-and-Scotch voice, all the while lighting one smoke after another.

"Listen, Dave," Judy said quietly for my ears only. She rested her hand on my arm. "I worry that the killer may have been in the act of removing your barber's body when you and Dolores walked in. You spot the body and say out loud he was your barber. I'm guessing here, but now he knows you were a customer. He gets a good look at you from cover near the body. If he did go into the shop to do business with your barber, maybe you were there waiting for a haircut, and he recognized you."

Aunt Rosalie turned from the front seat and looked at us. "Why are you whispering?"

"So you can't hear what I'm saying, mom." Uncle Art's guffaw stifled further questions.

"He knew the cops would question you," Judy resumed, leaning close to my ear. "You told me you identified Mike Budzik as being in the shop more than once. You said he's a killer. And killers stay alive and out of prison 'cause they observe their surroundings, even a kid waiting for a haircut, a kid who could maybe identify him, throw suspicion his way. You said the cops pulled this Budzik in for questioning."

I whispered in her ear which smelled nice. "Yes, but they let him go."

"OK, but please listen. If my guess is right, the killer's got the advantage. He knows you. But you don't know him, not for sure. But if he thinks you do, he won't think twice about killing you. That scares me, David."

Uncle Art watched us in the rearview mirror. "That's enough with the whispering," he said. "You're boring Dave with all our sinister secrets. Give him a break."

The beaches were crowded with July fourth celebrants, but Dad drove to the tip of the Peninsula which few families knew about or cared to drive that far for a swim. The rain drizzled on us the entire day as I recall, but it didn't dampen our fun. Judy's words did creep into my mind at times, but not often. The park closed at sunset, so we watched the fireworks from a golf course parking lot in the far west suburbs of Erie. It was one of those days you remember with smiles the rest of your life.

Uncle Art and family drove off for Pittsburgh the next morning. Judy and I didn't have much chance to talk before they left, but as we hugged good-bye, she did murmur, "Be careful."

Before Dad left to make sales calls in Meadville, he said now we could tell our friends about the move to Pittsburgh.

That afternoon, I walked over to Dolores's house. Dolores was lying on the lounge, reading the latest copy of *Seventeen*. She put down the magazine, but she didn't get up.

"Hello, David," she said in a colorless tone of voice.

"I missed you, Dolores. Did you have a good time at Chautauqua?"

"I suppose you could call it a good time," still flat.

"Hey! We beat Academy the other night. Jim Shea pitched, and I–"

"I read about it when we got back." This

wasn't going well. I jumped into the deep end.

"Listen, I've got something important to tell you. Dad's been promoted to district sales manager, and we have to move to Pittsburgh."

"Pittsburgh?" exclaimed Dolores, bolting upright. "You're kidding!"

"No, I'm not."

"When?"

"September."

"This September?" Dolores's voice got all trembly. I could tell she was on the verge of crying. "But it's your senior year. Why would they do that to us?" She began to sob. "Who will I go to the prom with if you're not here?"

"The prom? Don't you understand that after we move my chances of being with you will range from highly unlikely to never? I'm already missing you like crazy." Which wasn't entirely true, but her remark about the prom disturbed me. I wanted to hear her say she would miss me, too. It wasn't like we were packing up and leaving for southwestern Pennsylvania tomorrow.

"It isn't fair!" She was almost hysterical. Still no mention of my feelings about beginning a new school in a new town, or her feelings for me. "I hate your parents. They always ruin everything."

"Come on, Dolores. If you think they don't know how tough this will be for me, and Jeannie, too, you've got another think coming. What was Dad supposed to do, tell his boss to go fly a kite? Get real."

My guilt about making it with Cynthia disappeared. You never really can know another person completely, but when something happens that upsets the apple cart, you can find out a lot about someone's real feelings.

"Look, Dolores. We're both upset. We've got a week to think about this. Let's not say anything more. I'll call you next Saturday. Maybe we can go out to the peninsula to swim."

Dolores said nothing for a long time. She gazed off somewhere. Without changing her line of sight, she reached down and pulled up a handful of grass. She studied each blade, then slowly let them slip through her fingers.

She looked at me. I tried to read the meaning in her eyes without success.

"David, this bombshell you just exploded on me is a total shock. I'm sick and hurt and so mad at your parents I could . . . but it made me think about us in a different way, you know, what the future holds." She tossed *Seventeen* onto the grass. Here it comes, I thought.

"You're going to be gone in a couple of months. Who knows when we'll see each other again. No–" she stopped me from speaking, "let me finish. We really love each other, don't we?"

"Of course." Where was this leading?

She swung her legs to the side. "Here, sit beside me." She removed her sunglasses, looking earnestly at me with those wonderful blue eyes. "We've always talked about saving ourselves for each other, I mean making love. It almost happened that awful day two weeks ago." Dolores paused. "So, I want to make love with you. Today. Right now. You're going to be leaving before we know it, and this may be our only opportunity."

Of all the possible directions I thought her words would take, this wasn't one of them. She totally flabbergasted me. Her tone of voice came across with all the romance you might use to tell the milkman you want an extra quart of milk today. There wasn't any passion, any loving feeling in telling me she wanted to make love. God knows, I had tried to persuade Dolores to make love with me lots of times, and like she said, it darn near happened before Benny turned up lying practically next to us. There in that grassy spot behind Sonnhalter's, Dolores had wanted it as much as I did. And her voice and her eyes and the movement of her body told me so. But this invitation was a whole lot different.

"Dolores," I began, trying to find the exact right words to express what I was feeling, "Geez, Dolores, you know I'm crazy about you. And you know I've attempted to go all the way with you more than once since we've been going steady." The faint beginning of a puzzled frown began to work its way between her eyebrows. She hadn't expected a speech. I felt like I was floundering in twenty feet of ice water. "And I want to make love to you as much as ever. But... I gotta say that just now, the way you proposed this kind of surprised me, and not in a nice way either."

Dolores started to say something, but I took her hand, and said, "No, honey, let me finish. Maybe

I'm off base here, but you made it sound like some kind of business deal, like you were ordering me to do it with you." She was growing angry and tried to take her hand away, but I held tight.

"And something else bothers me," I went on. "You mentioned my moving away, and this might be our only chance, or words to that effect. Don't you see, it makes it sound like this is a one-night stand, and that's not what we're all about. If we make love, I want it to be part of our ongoing love for each other, not a once-in-a-lifetime treat."

This time she did pull away. Her mouth became a thin tight line, and her eyes showed how angry she was. "What ongoing love?" she snapped. "You're not going to be around next year. Do you have such a big ego that you believe we'll still go steady, that I'm going to enter a nunnery and wait around for you? I'm offering you one last chance to do it with me. Take it or leave it."

To tell the truth, I was feeling such a maze of emotions I didn't know which end was up. Why was I making a big deal about this? There had been no thought of ongoing love while I was making it with Cynthia. I had dreamed of making love with Dolores, and here she was, offering it to me on a silver platter, today, right now. And yet I knew if I let my hormones take over from my mind at that moment, it would be a bad mistake, and it wouldn't be even close to making love.

I stood. "I'm sorry, Dolores. You will never know how sorry I am."

I walked toward the gate to Chopka's, hoping any second she would call out that she was acting like a dope, and please come back, we need to talk, or something like that. But although I slowed down my steps to a crawl, she didn't say a word. I looked back when I got to the gate. Dolores was nowhere to be seen.

CHAPTER 8

A Close Call

The next couple of days weren't too great for me. I didn't say anything to my parents about the breakup. First off, what had transpired between me and Dolores wasn't any of their business. And I wasn't in the mood to talk about it with anybody. Shoot, given how my mother felt about Dolores, she would probably bake a cake to celebrate. The funny thing was that even though I was blue as all get out, I knew without a doubt that my response was absolutely the right one.

We closed out the regular baseball season by winning the remaining three games, and thoughts of Dolores didn't get in my way, thank goodness. The whole team focused on the approaching playoffs. At our final practice all the guys were sharp. I'm telling you, there were some rocket shots during batting practice, and not even Dickie made a bad throw to me in infield practice. Gil seemed impressed.

Things were moving fast on the home front. Dad needed to travel to meet his boss in Pittsburgh on the 13th, which also was my first playoff game against Tech. He felt really bad about the conflict, but there wasn't anything he could do to change it. Mr. Garland, Dad's boss, had arranged for Mother and Dad to meet with a real estate agent, so he suggested the family stay in Pittsburgh for the weekend and beyond.

Naturally, I wasn't about to miss a chance to be in the playoffs, so I'd be staying at home. After discussing the situation, Mother and Dad decided to ask his parents if they could stay with me. Under ordinary circumstances, I think my parents would have been okay with me staying home alone. I know my way around the kitchen, so there was no question of starvation or anything like that. But the Benny Angelone thing may have influenced their thinking. GrandDad and Grand-Mother Elliott agreed to take the Greyhound and would get to Erie next Wednesday so the family could drive to Pittsburgh Thursday.

I've mentioned that my Dad's parents were kind of strict. Actually, GrandMother was the one who saw everything as either black or white. GrandDad was another story. He had to choose his opportunities carefully, but he did chew Mail Pouch and drink a little whiskey when GrandMother wasn't in the vicinity. GrandDad loved to read, especially Zane Grey adventures. He'd sit for hours in his easy chair, one leg draped over the chair arm, head tilted back so he could look through his bifocals, mouth working, silently doing the dialogs. Last year, he introduced me to the works of Edgar Allen Poe and Henry Thoreau.

"Time you read something besides Captain Marvel comics, Dave," he said. "Those hero stories don't have educational value. You ought to be reading books that make you think; books that enlarge your understanding of yourself and others." He did read a wide range of literature, from Aeschylus to Zane Grey. That still impresses me.

I really enjoyed reading *Walden.* Thoreau built himself a neat little cabin in the woods near Walden Pond and spent two years there. He wasn't weird or a hermit. He had plenty of visitors. Thoreau thought he could learn about life out there. He wrote, "I wanted to live deep and suck out all the marrow of life." Man, that's what it's all about. That's how I want to live life. Every day a new adventure.

Dad and Jeannie picked up the grandparents at the bus station Wednesday evening. GrandDad had brought along a shopping bag of tomatoes and beans from his garden, which was like taking coals to Newcastle; Dad's garden was bursting with tomatoes and beans.

Next morning after breakfast, Dad packed the car and Mother gave instructions to her in-laws about the dos and don'ts of house rules, as though raising nine kids of their own hadn't prepared GrandMother and GrandDad for the likes of me. Then she told me what she and Dad expected of me, ending with a veiled reference to Dolores.

After they drove off, GrandDad toured Dad's garden and gave it the official seal of approval. What did he expect? Dad had learned his gardening skills from Granddad. While GrandMother tended to her knitting–she was making a baby outfit for my cousin, Ruthie, who was expecting the birth of her first child in October – GrandDad and I walked down to the lake. He didn't mention the murder, although I'm sure Dad had told him it happened near where we stood. We watched an ore carrier, smoke streaming from its funnel, steam around the tip of the peninsula, making for the channel into Presque Isle Bay.

GrandDad commented briefly how tearing up roots at this point of my life must be tough. He wasn't feeling sorry for me. He just stated a fact. "Sometimes the best adventures life offers come to us when we face difficulty and disappointment, Dave," he said. And that's all he said on the subject.

After supper, I put on my uniform. There were locker rooms at Ainsworth Field, but the Erie Sailors' minor league team didn't permit high school teams to use them. The plan was for me to ride my bike to Bobby Russell's house on East Avenue, then his dad would drive us across town to the park. I tied my spikes together and flipped them over the handlebars along with my Spalding 'Ferris Fain' first baseman's mitt. The grandparents weren't up for another bus ride, and Grandmother wasn't much of a baseball fan anyway, so they were staying home.

The early playoff game between Academy and Vincent went to the 11th inning before Academy finally scored the only run of the game. The field lights were already on as the ground crew smoothed the infield and relined the foul lines and batter's boxes. During warmups, the guys were acting cocky, trying to hide their nervousness. That wasn't good, so Bobby whistled and got us together back of first base. Gil started toward us, wondering what was going on, but Bobby waved him away. Then he talked in a calm way about Tech's pitcher, how to work on him, what to look for, stuff like that. Ted Duncan was pitching for us. Tech had two very good hitters, but our captain advised Duncan on the best way to handle them at the plate. Bobby was a sharp observer. His talk settled us down.

We won, 6-2. Dunc pitched a heck of a game, and we used Bobby's advice to get some timely hits off Tech.

After drinking a Coke with Bobby and Mr. Russell, I got on my bike for the long ride home. It was pretty late when I wheeled left off Lake Road onto Euclid. The battery on my headlight had died, so I nearly crashed into a car parked across the street from Benny's barber shop. My heart was still pumping hard when I heard the car start up. At first, I thought, he's probably mad because of how close I came to hitting the car. I hadn't scraped any paint or made any dents. I chided myself for jumping to a conclusion. As likely as not, the driver starting the car was coincidental.

But the car was moving up on me real slow, and when it got next to me, a spotlight fixed me in its beam. The light went out along with the headlights and the car stopped, engine idling. Before I had time to think how queer this was, the car roared to life, rushing right at me! I jumped the bike over the curb, lost control and fell onto the sidewalk. As I rolled over, I saw the car stop, then back up. I ran around the side of Kilgore's house and ducked into the shrubbery. The spotlight blazed, moving slowly back and forth along the houses. I was breathing so hard I was sure whoever was in the car could hear me.

The porch light switched on. The screen door

creaked, and Mr. Kilgore came out on his porch. The car moved off at a pretty fast clip. Mr. Kilgore said something to his wife as he went back into the house and closed both the screen and front doors. I stayed in the bushes for what seemed like an hour. I didn't know where the car went. He could be waiting for me somewhere on Fourth Street. Had he been parked at the corner watching for me because he knew I'd be riding home from the game?

I couldn't stay in the shrubbery all night. Staying low to the ground, I ran to my bike and pedaled home, really sprinting as I went under the streetlight at Fourth. I didn't use the brake until I was at the garage. I was trembling so bad my legs were rubbery. My breath came in short noisy gasps. After stowing the bike, I looked around the yard before going in the back door, but I couldn't see anyone. I waited until my system calmed down somewhat, then quickly got into the house. Judy's words echoed in my brain. "If the killer thinks you have what he's looking for, you could be in danger."

In my room, I sat at the secretary style desk and pulled down the hinged cover. My eyes went to the unfinished balsa wood model airplane I had never finished stowed in a cubbyhole. I quit building it six years ago because I gave up trying to do the next step.

You can't put this in a cubbyhole, I recall telling myself. *You can't sit on your butt wishing things had been different. This isn't a game; it's a fight, and this guy plays for keeps. If you're going to go down, go down swinging. Fight. How? Tell the cops. Let them handle it.* I closed the desk and stared at the wallpaper. Tell them what? I didn't have the license plate number. I couldn't identify the make and year of the car.

Sometime, just before sunrise, the time when most bad ideas are born, an idea not exactly loaded with good sense surfaced in my brain: The answer to this mess could be hidden somewhere in Benny Angelone's apartment or shop. I needed to get in somehow and thoroughly search the place. What would I be looking for? I had no idea, but I told myself I'd know it when I saw it.

I got out of my uniform and went to bed. I slept until GrandDad knocked, announcing breakfast would be ready soon. Great.

CHAPTER 9

David Finds a Clue and Quits a Job

After I dried the breakfast dishes, I made some excuse to my grandparents and walked up to Ernie's at the corner of Euclid and Lake Road. Ernie's grocery store fronted Angelone's barber shop. Once when I was getting a haircut, Ernie Niedermeyer had entered the shop through a door from his store into Angelone's. My plan was to hang around in the rear of Niedermeyer's until he was busy with a customer, then slip the bolt and go into the barber shop. I didn't know what to look for, but I figured the best place to look would be Benny's apartment.

It was as easy as 1, 2, 3. Mr. Niedermeyer had a big order of meat come in, and while he was dickering with the driver, I slid back the bolt and darted into the shop, quietly closing the door. With luck, Ernie wouldn't notice that the door was unlocked.

Being in Angelone's shop was kind of creepy, what with him being "bumped off" as they say in the movies. Fortunately, the door to the back room was unlocked. I knew no one would be in there, but I was nervous anyway. I closed the door and stood against it, surveying the territory. The room wasn't very large. A sink, stove, and small refrigerator were lined up on the wall to my right. The sun shone through the grimy window opposite the door, so there was enough light to see, and what I saw was a mess. Someone had ransacked the place. Furniture and lamps were overturned, drawers from Mr. Angelone's desk had been tossed around, papers, clothing, magazines, you name it, covered the floor.

The thoroughness of the search of Benny's place dampened my expectation of finding anything. Without planning anything, I waded in. No sense looking among the trash on the floor. I once heard one of Dad's friends say while they looked for a lost golf ball, "If you can't find something, look where you haven't looked before." Seemed sensible to me. I moved over to the kitchen area. All the dishes were smashed on the floor and the utensils had been dumped on the counter.

I opened the fridge. The food on the shelves had spoiled. The smell was as bad as baby vomit. My stomach is kind of delicate, and I had a hard time not throwing up. The ice cubes in the trays had melted because the power had been turned off. I shut the door and moved over to the stove. The oven was empty, and the drawer beneath the oven had been thoroughly examined. Nothing. "Come on," I said to myself, "where would you hide something you didn't want anybody else to see?"

Before I could answer my question, I saw Mr. Niedermeyer walk past the window. He never looked in. He was carrying a bunch of trash to the garbage cans behind the store. Soon enough he walked back, and again he never glanced at the window.

I walked over to the window, and pulled down

the shade, figuring if Mr. Niedermeyer made another trip past the window, he wouldn't be able to see inside the room. In retrospect, that didn't make a lot of sense – to assume he wouldn't notice the change to the window. Still, it was a good thing I did it. When the shade unrolled, something fluttered to the floor. Two sheets of lined paper evidently ripped from a small spiral-bound notebook had been rolled up in the window shade.

The words were hand-written, and the handwriting was difficult to decipher. Before I had worked through the first couple of words, I heard the sound of a door opening. My heart pounded. "Anyone in here?" said a voice. Mr. Niedermeyer had discovered the unlocked door to the barber shop. There was silence for what seemed like forever. Then the door closed, and there was the sound of the bolt being fastened.

I stuffed the papers in my pocket. How the heck was I gonna get out of here without Ernie seeing me? To leave by the shop door to Euclid was way too risky. Next to the sink was a door, which I assumed led to the garage. Maybe if my luck held, it would be unlocked. And sure enough, it opened when I twisted the knob. I pulled the door shut and stood on a landing a few steps above the garage floor. I waited until my eyes became accustomed to the dimness. Then I saw it: a key hung from a nail on the door frame. To my delight, it proved to be the key to the apartment. I put it into my pants pocket. Scrambling down the steps, I cautiously swung open the garage door. The coast was clear. I made a beeline for home.

There was no chance to examine the papers until after the supper dishes had been put away. I excused myself and retreated to my bedroom, hoping it wasn't too soon after supper, which might have aroused my grandparents' suspicions. They were in the habit of turning in early, so there was no problem. In my room, I opened the window, then spread the notebook papers on my bed. The information evidently had been written by Benny Angelone.

Insurance Expenses
8/9/48: P & W: $500
9/18/48: P & W: $500
10/13/48: P & W: $500

The monthly account continued like that until July of 1949. I figured P & W was his insurance agent, until I looked at the second piece of note paper. On the other piece of paper Benny had entered this:

7/8/49 JS phoned. P&W on the ropes. Everett Brown case, 1/3/48. W. bumped EB. Frame pins blame on WW. WW convicted, Western Pen.
7/16/49: accounts received: $800. P & W
8/21/49: received: $800. P & W

And so it went on, $800 a month until June of this year. I counted the months on my fingers. Twelve months at $800 smackers: $9,600! I rolled over on my back. 'P & W.' There was the P&W Newsroom on East Avenue. I sometimes rode there to see the baseball scores posted on a big scoreboard above their parking lot. I entered the store a few times to buy a bottle of pop. Beyond that I knew nothing of the place. It could've been a numbers drop, I had no way of knowing.

I went downstairs. GrandMother was asleep in the easy chair. GrandDad was reading a book. He looked up.

"I need to get the phone book from Dad's office. I need to find an address," I half-whispered. He nodded. Back upstairs, I scanned the Yellow Pages under P-Q. There were three establishments with the letters P and W in the name, but I dismissed them as possibilities. "Pauline & Wilma Beauty Parlor." "Peters and Wilson Funeral Home." "Pedals and Wheels Bicycles."

I studied the notes. P & W: it could refer to the names of individuals rather than businesses. I ruled out women's names. I began to write all the male first names beginning with either "P" or "W" I could think of but stopped after the first three or four. First names wouldn't be of any use. OK. Last names beginning with the letters "P" and "W." Individuals who have some connection to Benny Angelone. . . Pelinski and Washington! Detectives Pelinski and Washington? Are they P & W?

I stood and walked to the open window, peering into the dark night. The wind had picked up. To the northwest, far out over the lake, lightning flashed like a short-circuited illuminated sign. I closed the window. I picked up the notes, strode to the bed and sat. *"You're getting ahead of things,"* I thought. *"Their only known connection to Benny the barber is as inves-*

tigators of his murder. You have nothing concrete to link them to these notes."

Taking note of the framework of Benny's supposed involvement in the numbers racket, P and W could be two guys who found out Benny Angelone had crossed someone and shook him down. Then, Benny, thanks to an informant, had the goods on W for killing Everett Brown, and extorted P & W for a pile of dough. I stashed the notes in my desk and hit the hay. Just before sleep took me, a thought made me smile. With all this funny business going on, it was a wonder that my barber found time to cut hair.

I decided that a trip to the public library tomorrow would be a good idea. The newspaper archives might tell me what I needed to learn about Everett Brown's death.

Saturday morning held promise of being one of those special July days–blue sky, sunshine, soft breeze coming in off the lake. Great day for mowing Dr. Lawson's lawn. Great day to get together with Cynthia Lawson. Just the thing to get my mind off murder and danger.

Fortified by GrandMother's breakfast, I went to the garage to check my bike. Jumping the curb and laying down the bike to escape the guy who tried to run me down had caused some damage. The right pedal was bent, almost falling off: the headlight was missing, and the handlebars were twisted. I went to the cellar to grab some of Dad's tools and got to work.

It took a while, but I finally greased and attached the pedal. I wiped off my greasy hands. *Some-*

body wants me dead. But who? And why? The bolt that attached the handlebars to the frame was stubborn. I ran down to the cellar. Where the heck was the lubricating oil? There on the bottom shelf. *Benny's killer tore his apartment apart looking for something in there that would incriminate him.* I saturated the nut with oil. *It must be the notes I found. But that couldn't be the reason he tried to run me down. I didn't find those notes until yesterday afternoon.*

I fastened the crescent wrench onto the bolt and put my weight into it. Grudgingly it loosened. I lifted the handlebars out of the steering post. *If the killer thought I had written evidence against him, why try to run me down? That wouldn't do him any good. I wouldn't have kept the notes in my uniform. It made no sense. If I were dead, the evidence would still be out there somewhere.* Dad's woodworking vise would be too small to hold the metal bar. I laid the straight side of the handlebars flat on the grass, stood on it with both feet and slowly, cautiously pulled up on the bent part. After several inch-by-inch efforts, I set the bars into the stem, turned them 'til they were straight, and tightened the nut. The handlebars were fixed.

I walked up the street to the Kilgore's house. Maybe I'd get lucky and find the headlamp. Before I got to the corner, Joe Farrell's dog, Boots, jogged out to greet me, wagging the stub of its tail. I scratched behind his ears. He joined me the rest of the way. *Think, Elliott, I told myself. Maybe it isn't Benny's notes. Maybe it isn't anything in writing.* Mrs. Kilgore was watering the flowers in a window box. I told her my headlight had fallen off. She had found it under an azalea bush. I thanked her and turned for home, Boots at my heels. *Maybe it's something I saw or heard. Something which I didn't realize was important.* I stopped abruptly. *The killer knew he had to put me away before I figured it out.*

I took the bike for a short test. Everything seemed fine. I'd attach the headlamp later. After stowing the tools, I went upstairs to change my sweaty shirt and stuff.

Maybe if Dolores had called to apologize or to talk things out, I wouldn't have felt so charged up to see Cynthia. Dolores had not called. Yeah, I suppose it wouldn't have killed me to call her, but her words had made me feel like a broken bat instead of someone she said she loved. Deep down I knew it was over with Dolores.

I told my grandparents I had to mow Lawson's yard. GrandDad, who didn't miss much, asked, "Do you always take a bath before cutting grass?" His face was the picture of innocence.

Dr. Lawson's garage was empty. There was a good chance Mrs. Lawson, who also was his office receptionist, had left with him. Cynthia wasn't out in the yard, so I started in on the back yard. She would probably hear the mower reel hum or see me from a window. I finished the back, but no sign of Cynthia. Had she gone with her parents for some reason?
I knocked on the back door. Cynthia opened it, standing behind the screen. Boy, she looked terrific.

"David," she said, in a tone you might use if you saw a ketchup bottle sitting someplace you didn't expect it to be.

"Hi, Cynthia. You look wonderful," I said. "I finished the back. I was thinking we–"

"David," she interrupted in a quiet voice, "that's not going to happen."

"Oh," I mumbled, "your mother's home, huh?"

"Look, David," she went on, "You're a really nice kid, and I like you a lot. We enjoyed each other that one time, but I don't want to come between you and Dolores. Besides, I'm a little old for you."

"Don't worry about Dolores," I explained. "We broke up."

"I'm sorry, David. My mind's made up. You'll come to realize this is best. Take care of yourself." The door closed.

"Tell your Dad to get someone else to mow your damn grass!" I shouted.

CHAPTER 10

The Clue Confirmed?

Monday morning, GrandMother laid out a breakfast that would have prompted a farm hand to wave a white flag: thick slabs of bacon, fried eggs, about a half loaf of bread, fresh orange juice. GrandDad had taught all his grand kids to fry their bread in the hot bacon fat. I tore off a piece of the toast and dipped it in the fried egg yolk. The syrupy yolk merged with the warm, salty bacon-infused bread. Sensational.

Cynthia's rebuff surprised me and took the air out of my football. Why had she changed her attitude toward me in one week? I dipped another hunk of fried bread into the yolk. Why dwell on that? Cynthia taught me things about myself that I never imagined were a part of me. Being with her that afternoon meant something important. Not love: Intimacy. That morning I told myself I would never forget it. And I haven't.

While GrandDad washed the breakfast dishes, I dried, and GrandMother stowed them, the three of us discussed our plans for the day. GrandDad planned to hoe the garden for Dad. And GrandMother Elliott couldn't wait to clean the house. Mother was a good housekeeper, but GrandMother apparently felt she had fallen down on the job in certain areas. I smiled to myself. This was not the first time Grand-

Mother had gone over the house with white gloves. Mother never said anything about it, but that doesn't mean she was pleased to have her mother-in-law intrude on her household.

When I announced my intention to go uptown to the library to borrow some books, GrandDad beamed.

"Good idea, Dave," he said. "If you don't mind a suggestion?"

"No, GrandDad, of course not."

"You've been dealing with some heavy stuff for a while, so it seems to me some really humorous literature would be just the ticket. Ever hear of P.G. Wodehouse?"

"No, I haven't," I answered.

"Then you're in for a treat. See if they have *Young Men in Spats*. Great characters and laugh-out-loud short stories. Here," GrandDad said, "I'll write it down. I had a devil of a time locating him in our library, because I was spelling his name the way it sounds, which threw me off."

GrandDad Elliott's enthusiasm made me feel bad for not telling the real reason for my excursion to the Erie Library. But then I would have to tell them about Thursday night and going into Angelone's yesterday. They would have put the clamps on my plan right quick. I made a mental note to remember to take out the book he had recommended.

As I stepped off the bus at Perry Square to walk across the park to the library, it began to drizzle, and by the time I reached the library steps the rain was coming down rather hard. GrandDad wouldn't get much work done in the garden, I thought. Oh well, GrandMother would find something for him to do inside. Thinking about them nudged my memory to see if the library had that book GrandDad had recommended.

The woman behind the help desk pitched in to assist my search for information about the Everett Brown killing. "That was a very interesting crime," she said, friendly, but business-like. "Sit here at this table. It may take me a few minutes to get all the material together."

Public libraries are the best idea Andrew Carnegie ever had. From what I learned in Miss Bryant's history class, he had made zillions of bucks in the steel industry and most of the time treated his laborers like they were dog poop on his shoe. So, giving away some of his fortune to set up free libraries was the least Carnegie could do to make up for all that nasty stuff.

The library staff person was right: it took her some time to find what she was looking for. She came to the table carrying a stack of newspapers and set them in front of me. I thanked her and got to it. Benny Angelone's notes put the Everett Brown incident in early January 1948. I supposed it would be front page news, but I was wrong. It was a short piece on page 18 of the January 6 edition of the Daily Times.

According to the report, at approximately 4:30 p.m. Mary Etta Robinson, a Black woman who was walking past an alley off East 18th street noticed what she thought was a pile of clothing in the middle of the alleyway. She walked in a few steps to get a closer look and discovered it was the body of a Black man. Mrs. Robinson phoned the police, and Detectives Joseph Pelinski and Roland Washington, who were drinking coffee in a nearby restaurant, were dispatched to the scene. The corpse was identified as Everett Brown, 37, an ex-convict who had been involved in the Erie numbers racket. Mr. Brown had been shot once in the back. The news account mentioned that there had been a heavy snowstorm that day, and the victim's body was partially snow-covered. After identifying the dead man as Brown, Washington found a revolver buried in the snow. I looked out at the rain. *"Buried in the snow"?*

The next day's edition provided the information that police had determined that the murder weapon belonged to a guy who lived on 18th by the name of Willie Wilson. *Benny's WW?* The story mentioned that Wilson had stolen candy and cigarettes from a neighborhood store in 1940 when he was ten years old but hadn't done anything illegal since, or if he did, he wasn't caught. A police spokesman was asked why Wilson had bruises on his face and a cast on his left arm. He explained that "Willie had a bad temper and put up a fight" when police arrested him. After two weeks in jail, Willie Wilson signed a confession that he had shot Everett Brown.

At Wilson's trial several months later, his lawyer asserted that Willie had been exhausted and confused and had signed that confession under duress. Willie testified that he had never owned a gun and had never even touched a gun in his life. But the jury believed what Pelinski and Washington said at the trial, and Willie was found guilty of manslaughter and sentenced to eight years in Western Penitentiary. The newspaper accounts and the notes Benny Angelone wrote persuaded me that Pelinski and Washington were 'P & W'.

Benny's notes said JS phoned him in July 1949, evidently with proof that the real shooter of Everett Brown was W, very likely Roland Washington. The key to proving this was JS. I reread the stories. Nobody with those initials was mentioned in any of the news accounts. I rubbed my ear. There were lots of unanswered questions. Who is JS and what's his connection to Benny Angelone? And how did this JS know the real story? More important, why didn't JS tell Wilson's lawyer? Maybe JS didn't find out the truth until after the trial. If JS told the true story to the district attorney now, wouldn't that get Willie Wilson released from the penitentiary?

Two disturbing thoughts came to me. What if Pelinski and Washington found out JS knew the real scoop, and silenced him? I had assumed they questioned Dolores and me to find Angelone's killer. But what if they killed Benny Angelone to erase all witnesses and then questioned us to find out if we had seen anything that could connect them to his murder?

I sat there in the library, watching the rain through the window, trying to decide what to do. Even though I was sure Pelinski and Washington were

P & W, there was no proof. It could be a coincidence that they were the cops who investigated Brown's murder. As much as I hated to admit it, the idea they killed Brown was only circumstantial evidence. P&W could stand for Pete and Wayne, or whoever.

On the other hand… I assumed Benny's killer had ransacked his apartment to find the P & W notes. But he couldn't know for certain Benny had kept an account of the payments and the reason for them unless Benny told him. Which was highly unlikely. Following that line of thought, it seemed improbable that the attempt on my life was related to the notes. I stretched my arms, then leaned my chin on my right hand. An idea slowly took shape that became a belief: the killer raked over the apartment to find something he knew was there or should be there --- unless he concluded someone else had found it.

Wait: what if he thinks I found whatever it is? Is that why he tried to run over me and make it look like a hit and run? That made no sense. OK, so I'd be dead. However, what I supposedly had found still was out there and could be used against him. I tried to make sense out of all this, but it was like trying to untangle a fishing line.

I returned to the search for JS. Maybe there would be something in the January 1950 editions. The woman at the help desk cheerfully complied with my request, and soon I had all the January editions. My hunt for JS was unsuccessful, but there were some interesting stories that caught my attention. None were more intriguing than the sensational news in the

January 18 papers that some guys had stolen $3 million from a Brinks security company in Boston. This had nothing to do with what I was looking for, but I made a mental note to read the story on my next trip to the library.

"The library closes in ten minutes," the help desk woman told me. "Are you finished with the papers?"

Yes, ma'am," I said. "Thanks for your help." As I handed her the papers, I noticed a small piece of paper clipped to the first page of the January 1st edition. I asked her what the apparently random series of numbers, letters and symbols meant.

"That's our filing code. Unless you're on the staff, it doesn't mean anything to library patrons." I checked out *Young Men in Spats* and walked through the rain to the bus stop. It was clear to me that I was in deep water here. What the heck did I know about murder investigations?

I had to stand in the aisle 'til the bus got to East Avenue. I looked absently at the ads above the windows. "Learn The Morse Code in 10 Days!" one guaranteed. The words of the library staff woman came back to me. "Unless you're on the staff, it doesn't mean anything to library patrons." A light switched on in my brain. Suppose Benny's killer were looking for some object, something that wouldn't raise an eyebrow among the general public if found but would immediately be recognized as damning evidence by an individual who was "on the staff," so to speak?

The light inside my head became blinding. The

killer wants me dead because he believes I'm "on the staff," that I found what he was searching for, and understood its implication! A pain began to grow in the back of my head, and for the first time, I noticed I was sweating to beat the band. I was so preoccupied, a lady had to tap me on the arm and show me there was an empty seat next to her. This line of thought racing through my mind may have answered a question that had bugged me. Why hadn't the killer come after Dolores? She was with me when we found Mr. Angelone. The cops questioned her. He had no reason to do anything to her because I was the one on the staff, I was the one who was dangerous to him, not Dolores. Just in the nick of time I pulled the rope to stop at Euclid. Nuts! The bus was pulling away. I sprinted after it and rapped on the folding doors. The driver braked and opened the door.

"Sorry, sir. I left a book on the seat." I retrieved it, not looking at the smiling passengers. "Thanks."

The rain had stopped. At least I wouldn't get soaked walking home.

When I crossed to the other side of East Lake Road, I backtracked to Sanford and headed home that way, just in case someone was waiting on Euclid to make sure I didn't get home. As I hurried along, I kept a close eye on the Lake Road traffic. Walking down Sanford, I remembered that late afternoon when I picked up Dolores walking this very same sidewalk. It seemed like it was a million years ago. One sentence she spoke that day came back to me: "If you hadn't come along, I'd be home and none of this would have happened to me." Yeah, Dolores, I wish I hadn't come along that day. None of this would have touched my life either. But I did pick you up. Now I have to deal with what happened and find out who killed Mr. Angelone before he kills me. Supposing my latest brainstorm was at least partly correct, what did the killer think I found, and why does he think I figured out what it meant?

The game was on the line. I was at bat. I had two strikes on me and no clue as to when and where the next pitch would arrive.

CHAPTER 11

Strike Out and Watch Out

Tuesday the weather was spectacular, which happens often after a day of rain. Great day for our playoff game against Academy. GrandDad said he was going to finish working in Dad's garden, since he'd been rained out yesterday. I asked if he wanted my help, but he said no. GrandMother said she still had some cleaning to finish up. I hoped she wouldn't ask me to run the vacuum cleaner. She didn't.

I went into Dad's office to phone Dolores, thinking maybe we could at least talk things over, but there was no answer. I sat there for a while, messing with the plastic letter opener before returning it to the ink blotter. I reached in my pocket and took out the Cracker Jack charm Dolores gave me on our first date: a silver plastic baseball mitt with a bat and ball across the pocket. We went to the movies that evening at the Avenue Theater and shared a box of Cracker Jack. That was last July. I had carried that in my pants pockets for a year. We had some fun times; the dance at the "Y" when she taught me how to polka; walking home from school during a heavy snowstorm, and Dolores making us cocoa when we got to her house.

I started to put the charm in my side pocket but laid it on the ink blotter. In all likelihood, my rejection of her proposition marked the end of our relationship. I was still convinced it had been the right thing to do. That doesn't mean I had no regrets. I picked up the Cracker Jack token, walked to the kitchen and dropped it in the trash can under the sink.

I paged through the morning paper, not expecting to find any answers to Benny's murder, or any of the other situations surrounding the case. I turned to the sports page, looking for an article about the high school playoff games, but there was only a notice of the teams who were playing: Tech vs. Strong-Vincent 6:00 p.m., Academy vs. East approximately 7:45 p.m. I reorganized the paper so Granddad could read it later.

As I placed it on the coffee table, I noticed the headline on a brief article at the bottom of the first page: Coudersport Bandits Convicted. I picked up the paper and read:

Stanley "Gus" Gusciora and Joseph "Specs" O'Keefe, both of Boston, Mass., were convicted of the robberies of Harley's Gun Shop in Kane, Pa., and Rosenbloom's Men's & Boys' Clothing Store in Coudersport, Pa. Gusciora has been remanded to the McKean County Jail for sentencing. O'Keefe remains in Bradford County Jail in Towanda. Dates for sentencing have not been set, pending appeals by the defendants' attorneys."

I'll bet Mother will be hearing from her cousin Mabel about this, I thought. This story would be headline news in the Coudersport Endeavor. Coudersport didn't have much to get excited about, except maybe somebody bagging a 12-point buck during deer season.

In the early playoff game Prep smeared Strong-Vincent. If we beat Academy, we'd face Prep in the semifinals. If we beat Academy.

Shea was pitching for Academy. We talked before the game, wishing each other luck. Before we headed for our dugouts, Shea said, "tonight's my night, Ellie. You got the best of me in the last game, but not tonight. Nothin' personal, pal." He grinned, punched me in the arm, and ran to his dugout on the third base side before I had a chance to reply.

The game's play-by-play isn't important, except to say that Lukey and Shea both pitched terrific baseball. Finally, in the top of the ninth, Academy's center fielder Tommy Wisner led off with a triple. Big Lukey struck out the next batter, but the next guy hit a fly ball to right-center field. Mel Cabeloff made a great running catch and threw home. Tommy beat the throw. 1-0 Academy, and that's how it stood as we came up for our last at-bat. Coach Gil spoke to the team in the dugout as Shea threw his warmups. "Okay, now," said Gil, "let's be smart hitters. We can do this. Don't swing at first pitches, Okay? Make him pitch to you."

At first, it worked like clockwork. The first batter walked. Playing for the tie, Gil had the next hitter lay down a sacrifice bunt. One out, but we had the tying run in scoring position. But Shea struck out the next batter. Two outs. I could see Shea's confidence growing. But Bobby Russell scratched a single to the infield, and we had the tying run on third.

I stepped into the batter's box. I flashed a smile at Shea, but he didn't return it. He just nodded, all business. His first pitch, a fastball, was outside, and his next pitch, a sharp-breaking curve, was located in a spot where I couldn't do anything with it. Strike one. I got hold of his next pitch, another curve, but it was foul by five yards. Jim threw another curve for ball two. Two and two. I stepped out of the batter's box and rubbed some dirt on my hands. Shea was standing behind the mound, looking out to center field.

Finally, both of us were ready. In that brief moment before he took the stretch, I knew Shea was going to throw his fastball. I set up a little deeper in the box, where I'd have a split second more to get around on his fastball. Too late I realized Jim had pitched another curve which looked nice and fat, right over the plate until it dropped beneath my swing. Game over. End of the playoffs for us.

I met my friend halfway between the pitching mound and home plate. "Great game, Shea," I said, and I meant it. "I never expected four curves in a row."

"Yeah, I know," he chuckled. "We're even, huh?"

"Yeah," I said with a rueful smile. "We're even. See you in church, I'll be rooting for you to beat Prep."

As Bobby and Mr. Russell and I walked to their Chevy, I saw a big car pull out of the parking lot. No mistaking the shape: 1950 Cadillac. *So what*, I told myself. *There's more than one '50 Caddy in Erie.* Nevertheless, I wasn't looking forward to the bike ride home from Russell's house. The only road home was East Lake Road. No way to alter my route. But I did decide I would get off on Sanford instead of my street.

A switch engine was moving across the Hammermill bridge as I rode underneath. The vibration set in motion by the engine apparently shook loose a big hunk of concrete, which landed with a heavy thump close beside my bike, scaring me to death. Pieces of concrete sprayed along the road. If that chunk had hit me . . .! I parked my bike on the median strip and went back and threw the biggest pieces off the road. Bobby Carney's Dad worked at Hammermill, and he told Dad not to drive under the bridge when a train was going across, because lots of times it dislodged hunks of gravel and concrete. Mr. Carney was so right.

My headlight had crapped out again, so I decided to ride the sidewalk the rest of the way. My breathing had almost returned to normal, and my legs were working again as I passed the entrance to Lakeside Cemetery. I saw something out of the corner of my eye. A black 1950 Cadillac was parked against the gates, facing the road! I stood on the pedals for a block, banging over the curbs of side streets, looking back over my right shoulder, but there was nothing. I arrived home without incident. My throat was raw, and I hadn't yet caught my breath as I shut the garage door. I bent, putting my hands on my knees, my lungs laboring.

GrandDad's voice came out of the darkness of

the backyard. "You OK?" he asked. Boy, he scared me! He moved out from under the Maple tree.

"Yeah," I gasped. "Just... tried... to... make... it... home... in... ten... minutes." There was a sound of spitting. GrandDad had sneaked out back to fire up a chew of Mail Pouch.

"Hmm," he observed, "seems a little dumb, riding in the dark without a headlight as if a demon was chasing you." He plucked the chaw of tobacco from his cheek and tossed it up on the garage roof. "How'd the game go? Did you win?"

"Uh-uh," I managed, still winded.

"Sorry about that." GrandDad made no move to go inside. "Your hell-bent-for leather ride wouldn't have anything to do with that barber's murder, would it?" I pretended I was still out of breath, buying time before I replied. Not much got past my grandfather.

I walked over to the back steps and sat. He sat next to me. There was a faint aroma of tobacco about him. I wanted to tell him everything, but decided not to. "GrandDad," I began, "I struck out with the tying and winning runs on base. We're out of the playoffs. I just had to ride as fast as I could to get the anger and sadness out of me."

"That's too bad, David. That had to hurt." GrandDad said. He went on, "But I didn't just fall off a turnip truck. Why don't you just tell me the real reason you came flying in here." We sat without speaking for a time. I was turning things over in my mind. Somewhere over on Eagle Point Boulevard a dog barked. This business was becoming too big a load for me to carry alone. I needed to confide in someone with common sense. Someone who wouldn't betray a confidence. I told him everything, including my theory about being "on the staff".

He said nothing until I finished. "Do your parents know all this?"

"No, just the part when I found the body. Most of the later stuff happened since they went to Pittsburgh."

The back door opened behind us. "For heaven's sake," said GrandMother, "are you two going to sit out there all night?"

"We'll be there in a bit," said GrandDad. "Why don't you go up to bed? I'll lock up."

"Don't keep David up all night telling your stories. The boy needs his rest." She closed the door without waiting for his reply.

"You're in a dangerous predicament, son. With regard to those notes, I'd say that under other circumstances, your best plan of action would be to tell the police. From what you've told me those two detectives may be the primary suspects. The district attorney would be the best person to contact. His office handles cases of police corruption." GrandDad stopped talking, but I figured he had more to say.

"Here's what I'm thinking, David. I doubt that the notes have anything to do with the attempt on your life the other night. And maybe P&W had nothing to do with Mr. Angelone's death. We can't be absolutely sure that block of concrete didn't fall from the bridge accidentally. It could be a coincidence. And the car you saw may not be the same Cadillac you saw at the pumping station just before you stumbled onto Angelone's body. But to my way of thinking It's better to assume that tonight you were a target for a second time, and I think it's the man who killed Mr. Angelone. It's obvious he knows your routine and has a good idea of where you are most of the time."

He stood up and walked a few feet into the grass. I could barely see his form in the moonless night. "Have to stretch my legs," GrandDad explained. "Let's walk to the back of the garage." Our short stroll spooked Pete, our next-door neighbor's cat, who was hunting mice. The neighborhood was shutting down for the night. Most of the houses over on Sanford were dark. The Big Dipper was tipping over in the sky above us. A peaceful summer's night. The scene did nothing to dissipate the fear churning my brain and my gut.

"Assuming your barber's killer wants you dead and has staged the attempts as an accidental death, your notion that he believes you found something you know would incriminate him seems credible. Here's the rub: It doesn't matter whether or not you found the unholy grail he has to have. He believes you did. For that reason he's going to keep after you until he finishes you.

"So, what you're getting at is it's unlikely that Budzik or Pelinski and Washington are the ones who are trying to kill me, right?"

"Well, that's the way it seems to me. 'Course, I could be wrong. Let's go in. The night air is waking up my arthritis." As we walked back to the house, Grand-

Dad said, "Look, David, I won't tell anyone what you told me, but in my opinion you need to tell your dad. Maybe he knows someone, an attorney, the owner of a company he does business with, someone who has a lot of influence in the city or the county, or better yet, the district attorney. You need protection, and," he grabbed my arm in a vice grip, "you must drop the Ellery Queen stuff."

"Okay, GrandDad," I said, without conviction. Before he and I got inside the house that night, I made a decision. I was fed up with being a sitting duck. Some coach or general once said that the best defense is a good offense. Or was it the other way around? My "good offense" would concentrate on doing stuff behind the scene. First, fill Dad in on recent events, and make an appointment to show the district attorney the notes I found in Benny's apartment. Then, library research: reading everything I could find on Benny Angelone's involvement in numbers gambling: who are some of the other players in Erie? How many of them did Benny know? Is there any hint that someone had tried to take over Benny's territory or vice-versa? I wouldn't take stupid and unnecessary chances. But I was more determined than ever to find out who killed Benny the barber, and why.

Although I was a naive kid without experience in this, and some of my questions were unlikely to find answers in the newspapers, there was always a possibility of learning something.

CHAPTER 12

Dead Men Do Tell Tales

The family arrived home from Pittsburgh late afternoon in the midst of the worst storm of the summer. The rain hammered against the windows like machine gun bullets, and the lightning and thunder blasted repeatedly. My grandparents and I stood in the sunroom, watching as the four travelers waited for a chance to beat it onto the front porch. Finally, Mother opened her door and jumped out, moving right quick for an old woman, then Jimmy and Jeannie piled out of the back seat and Dad slid across the front seat and dashed to the porch, smacking into Jimmy, who, for reasons known only to himself, had stopped at the top step. No one was hurt, although from the howl my brother made you'd have thought Dad had laid a mortal blow on him. It was funny, if you were just watching. Even GrandMother laughed. We're such a dignified family. I was happy to see them after a week-long absence though, even my sister and brother.

Everybody seemed to talk at the same time and at the top of their lungs. "We had a nice visit with Art and the family," Dad announced, while Jeannie tried to tell me something she saw at the Carnegie Museum and Jimmy yelled about the steep hills and the big barges on the river. It wasn't until we were seated at the table for supper when Mother announced that they had found the perfect house in Mount Lebanon not too far from Uncle Art, and we were going to move August 21. Only four weeks away.

The talk around the table was brisk and exciting. This and that had to be done, friends had to be called, stuff had to be sorted and packed, and so on and so forth. I wasn't listening because I was thinking that back in June when Mother and Dad told us we would be moving to Pittsburgh, my reaction was that it was the end of the world. Tonight I was glad we were moving. In fact, I wished we were moving tomorrow. The sooner I didn't have to look over my shoulder for a black Cadillac or the possibility of running into Pelinski and Washington or "Fat Stuff" Budzik the better.

Next morning Dad drove his parents to the Greyhound Bus depot, and I rode along. The early morning fog was lifting, but a steady drizzle required the windshield wipers to do their stuff. The library was just across Perry Square from "the Big Dog House," Jim Shea's term for the Greyhound bus station. The Pittsburgh bus was boarding when we pulled into the parking lot. I thanked my grandparents for staying with me, and managed to exchange a special wink with GrandDad.

"Bye David," he said, smiling. "Don't take any wooden nickels."

"I'll try not, GrandDad. Thanks for introducing me to P.G. Wodehouse."

After the bus headed out, I told Dad I wanted to do some work in the library and would take a bus home in the afternoon. His face held a quizzical expression, but he only said he'd tell Mother, to be careful, and did I have bus fare. I was pretty sure GrandDad had kept his promise about not saying anything about the two incidents, so I figured Dad's cautionary warning was just routine.

He dropped me off in front of the library.

"Dad, I know you're really busy getting ready for the move and all, but do you think you and I could have a private talk tonight? I have some things I need to tell you." He agreed, saying it wouldn't be a problem.

The drizzle had become a gentle rain. There would be no pickup game of baseball in the neighborhood today. A good day to spend in the library. Maybe luck would be with me, and the newspapers would provide the identity of the mysterious JS.

There was a different lady at the Help Desk. I wrote down the dates of papers I figured might be the most likely to have something about JS. As an afterthought, I asked for copies of the January 18th, 19th, and 20th of 1950. I wanted to learn more about the big Brinks robbery in Boston. As the Help Desk lady handed me the newspapers, I asked her if she could tell me how I could find the name of the district attorney and where he had his office.

"His name is Robert Barnes," she said. "I believe his office is in the County Courthouse over on West Sixth Street. Let me get the address." In a minute she returned. "The Courthouse is at 146 West Sixth. District Attorney Barnes's office is in room 100, first floor."

I thanked her and slid the top newspaper from the stack. The search for JS became tedious and produced no results.

I reread the short article about Everett Brown's killing and the subsequent trial of Willie Wilson but no JS was mentioned. I pushed the papers aside.

Did it really matter if I discovered the identity of JS? Benny's notes revealed evidence that Willie Wilson didn't shoot Everett Brown. Based on that, the district attorney might reopen an investigation into the Everett Brown killing. The smart thing for me to do was to drop this on Mr. Barnes's desk. He'd know how to deal with this. I glanced at the clock. Only twelve-thirty. If I'd remembered to bring along Benny's notes I could have taken them to the District Attorney and been done with this.

I picked up the story about the Brinks robbery. The account of the daring robbery fascinated me. Reading the newspaper accounts that rainy afternoon, I began to admire the thorough planning those crooks had done. They seemed to have thought of everything. Nobody got hurt, either, which was cool. I turned to page nine to finish the story. And there in a paragraph near the bottom of the page, was an eye-witness account by one of the Brinks guards who had been tied up. He said that all the gang members wore rubber Halloween masks of a comic book character to conceal their faces.

I pushed my chair away from the table and walked to the window. I concentrated on everything that had happened since Dolores and I stumbled upon Mr. Angelone's body. In light of what I had just read, one brief incident in Angelone's Barber Shop came back to me. I replayed the scene in my head. Back at the library table I reread the Brinks story.

Was Benny Angelone's murder somehow connected to the Brinks robbery? Did he know the names of the Brinks gang? But wait a minute: how could he? How in the world could a barber in Erie, Pennsylvania know the identities of the gang who stole more than $2 million from a Brinks garage in Boston? I didn't see how Benny could find out what the FBI hadn't been able to in all those months.

Okay, suppose Angelone somehow did get hold of the names of the gang. Why wouldn't he pass this information to the FBI and claim the $100,000 reward? The more I thought, the more questions showed up.

I walked back to the window. My thoughts were ricocheting in my head like the metal ball in a pinball arcade game. All at once the rebounding stopped. Well, slowed down would be more accurate. All the questions seemed to fade away, and I knew what had to be done. I hurried down the Library steps and ran to the bus stop at the corner.

That evening, Dad and I talked behind the closed door of his office. He listened to my narrative of the close calls and my resolve to stop taking risks and thinking I was tough guy Philip Marlowe. Without explanation I told him Dolores and I had broken off our relationship. I deliberately omitted the part about my surreptitious entry into the barbershop and apartment. Dad thanked me for confiding in him. He forbade me to even think about doing any more freelance detective work.

I didn't sleep well that night. My mind was in overdrive, and I couldn't seem to shut it down. I was more than a little bleary-eyed when I joined the family for breakfast. I helped myself to orange juice, piled some Wheaties and milk in a bowl and sat at my usual place. The talk was all about moving to Pittsburgh.

One thing for sure, Jeannie had been won over. She couldn't stop talking about how *big* Pittsburgh is, and the rivers and the steep hills, and the skyscrapers and riding the incline to the top of Mt. Washington, and so on and on. I can't say I listened closely, but I tried to nod and say things like, "Wow!" or "That sounds great!" at the appropriate time.

I waited for a lull in the conversation so I could tell Mother and Dad my plans for the day. I had rehearsed my speech while scrubbing my teeth that morning. The story seemed plausible to me. I didn't think it would arouse their suspicions.

Dad picked up the morning paper, and Mother went to the stove to get another cup of coffee. Jeannie and Jimmy went off somewhere in the house. I dove in.

"Dad, I forgot to tell you that while you were in Pittsburgh, the district attorney called me." Dad lowered the paper. Mother almost dropped her cup.

"The district attorney called you?" asked Dad,

raising his eyebrows. "What did he want from you?"

"He wanted me to come to his office this morning so he could ask me some questions about Mr. Angelone's murder. Actually, he didn't call, his secretary did."

"You <u>forgot</u>?"

"What's his name?" Mother wanted to know.

"Uh, Robert Barnes."

"Barnes," said Dad with some disgust in his tone of voice. "I didn't vote for him. Too darn liberal for my taste."

"I just knew this mess hadn't ended," Mother said. "Harold, you need to go with him."

"Em, I can't cancel my trip to Dunkirk Radiator. I've been working to get their business for almost a year. The purchasing agent is a stickler for keeping appointments. Short of a death in the family, he wouldn't take kindly to a postponement."

"What could he possibly want to know that you haven't told those two detectives?" Mother wondered.

"I don't know. The woman didn't say."

Dad chimed in, "My guess is there's been some new development in the case, and they want you to go over your experience that day. Maybe you'll think of something you didn't consider important back then. I know you'll handle this just fine. Just tell them what you know, and don't add your opinions or conjectures."

"Okay, Dad. That's good advice."

Soon after this exchange, Dad said goodbye

and drove off on his way to Dunkirk. As we were doing the breakfast dishes, it was Jeannie's turn to wash. Jeannie was really fast at washing dishes, and there was a pile of them waiting for me to dry. She would finish before I got to the silverware. I slipped a plate into the soapy water.

"That's not clean," I said.

"Yes, it is," Jeannie said with annoyance.

"Oh-oh. Here's another one," and a second dish disappeared beneath the bubbles.

"Mother!" she yelled.

Without coming into the kitchen or waiting to hear the rest of Jeannie's complaint, Mother said, "David stop putting clean dishes back in the sink."

I was still drying the frying pan and the coffee pot when Jeannie finished scrubbing the sink. She dried her hands, stuck out her tongue, and sauntered from the kitchen.

My chore for the day finished, I headed out the door for the bus stop at the corner. In my pants pocket were Benny's notes, and the key to his apartment door. After giving the notes to District Attorney Barnes, I planned to search the barber shop. I couldn't shake the notion that Benny Angelone had hidden something which would answer the questions about his possible connection to the Brinks job.

The Erie County Courthouse building on West Sixth looked like a Greek temple. Twin buildings complete with six fluted Corinthian columns flanked the main entrance, forming a U-shaped facility. Huge wooden doors indicated that serious business happened inside, and you'd best not forget it. I tugged open the door and entered the marble hallway. A receptionist directed me to Room 100.

As I approached the door to Mr. Barnes's office, it occurred to me that without an appointment he was not likely to see me or anyone who just dropped in. I needn't have worried. When I told the receptionist I was David Elliott, and that I needed to see Mr. Barnes about the Angelone killing, she picked up the phone, and in less than a minute I was sitting by his desk. The district attorney was tall, had curly hair, and wore a bow tie, and not one of those fake clip-ons either. He came around the desk, his hand out. We shook, and he said, "Nice to meet you, David. I'm glad you came in. Finding the body of Mr. Angelone was a nasty experience."

"Yes sir, it was. That's why I came to see you. The detectives who questioned me that evening were Sergeant Joe Pelinski and his partner, Roland Washington. They haven't contacted me since, but the paper said that they're still the officers charged with leading the investigation. Is that right, Mr. Barnes? And do I have it right that they were the first officers at the scene of Everett Brown's murder in 1949?" He nodded, prompting me to continue.

I fished the notes from my pocket. "My granddad said you're the one who ought to have these."

He read the notes, then read them again

"Where did you get this?" I told Mr. Barnes the whole story, but not before he called his secretary to copy my statement. When I finished, he smacked his hand on the desk.

"What the hell did you think you were doing? Don't you know you could have gotten yourself killed?" I began to think giving him the notes was a huge mistake.

"Do your parents know you broke into Mr. Angelone's place and found this? Have you told anyone at all?"

"No sir, they don't. My granddad's the only one who knows about all this."

"These notes contain significant information about the Everett Brown murder and the Wilson trial and conviction. If the wrong people had discovered you found them, chances are you wouldn't be sitting here. My staff will investigate this and if what you have shared is what it appears to be, we have a major criminal case on our hands. You may be involved in the investigation as a material witness, and if there is an indictment of these two individuals, It's possible the prosecutor will want your testimony if the case goes to trial, which is very likely.

"You are not to share the details of this meeting with anyone except your parents. Also," he continued, "until we have verified the truth of this information and arrested the suspects, you may be in grave danger. Although there's no hard evidence to indicate that P&W are Pelinski and Washington, you can be certain that if either of them contacts you, it will not be on my orders or those of the chief of police. If they do call or show up, here's my direct phone number. Don't waste time: call immediately."

I appreciated District Attorney Barnes's concern and his insistence that I call right away if Pelinski or Washington came around. But given the circumstances of the attempts on my life, what good would having his number have been?

Mr. Barnes stood up, signaling that the meeting was over. He stepped around the desk and shook my hand. "Thank you, David. You did the right thing by bringing this to me. My people will get to the bottom of this, and then you'll have nothing to worry about." He pointed at me. "And you stay out of this. Understood?"

"Yes, sir."

The district attorney left the room. His secretary asked for my address and phone number and told me someone from the office would be contacting me.

As I walked the corridor to the front door of the Courthouse that morning in late summer of 1950, two thoughts occupied my mind. Was there a connection between the murder of Benito Angelone and the Brinks robbery in January? What about those Halloween masks, and the conversation I overheard between Angelone and that tough-looking stocky guy? I had discovered by a fluke that Benny kept notes on things that were critical to him and was clever about hiding them. The key to his apartment was in my pocket. If the coast was clear, my next stop would be to search Angelone's barber shop.

The second thought was how to tell my parents the rest of the story. I climbed aboard the Lawrence Park bus and sat in the last row. Dad and Mother undoubtedly knew the district attorney wouldn't have summoned me to a meeting unless something big had happened. When Dad got back from Dunkirk this evening, there would be lots of difficult questions requiring difficult honest answers.

I couldn't see any way around telling the truth that I had initiated the contact with Mr. Barnes. That meant telling them about going into Mr. Angelone's place and finding the notes. When they heard this, they would put the clamps on me, ending my attempt to find out who killed my barber. I had discovered that I enjoyed trying to solve his murder. I realized in that eureka moment six years ago, that this fascination would be a part of me for a long time.

The bus dropped me at the corner of Euclid. I peered through the window of Ernie's Red & White. Ernie had no customers in the store that I could see, in spite of the sign in the window advertising a special price for hot dogs. I walked around to the side of the store and pretended to tie my shoe on the step to the barber shop. I checked out the scene. The shade was pulled down on the large window next to the entrance door, blocking the view from the street. The door was covered with newspaper. Great.

When I got to the garage I looked around but saw no one. The garage door was unlocked, and I hustled in, closing the door. After my eyes got used to the darkness, I tip-toed up the three steps to the apartment door and stood listening for about a minute. Nothing. My hands were shaking. I almost dropped the key. The apartment was in the same mess as before. Nobody had been here since my visit; a good sign. I slowly slid open the bolt on the door to the shop and went in.

As far as I could tell, nobody had been in there for some time. Unlike Benny's apartment, nothing was out of place. It was warm and stuffy, as if all the air had been used up, and sweat began to bead on my face and arms. Angelone's was a typical neighborhood barber shop: one barber chair, customer chairs against one wall, a big mirror behind the barber chair, a counter which held a jar filled with blue liquid and a couple of combs. Also on the counter were a hand mirror, a mug of dried and cracked shaving soap with a shaving brush on a little stand, a box of tissues Benny would put around your neck before he snapped on the cloth to keep off the hair, and an assortment of hair tonics and aftershave colognes.

Under the counter were drawers where he stored towels and similar items. There was a Mack Truck pin-up calendar on the wall, featuring Miss July. I opened the drawers one by one, looking for something out of the ordinary, but there were only towels, three straight razors, and two electric clippers. Next, I leafed through the comic books and magazines, Superman, Batman, Popular Mechanics, True Crime Stories, Field and Stream, stuff like that. No loose pages, no notes scribbled in the margins. I got down on the floor and looked at the undersides of the customer chairs. Nothing but dried wads of chewing gum.

Maybe there was nothing here. I dusted my

pants and sat in the barber chair. If I was Benny Angelone and I had to hide a page from a notebook or a typewritten message, where would be the best place? The ceiling fan blades! I grabbed the broom standing in the corner and pushed the fan blades, brushing the broom on top of the blades, hoping to feel something attached. After nearly dropping the broom on the floor it was obvious there wasn't anything up there except dust. I returned the broom to its place in the corner next to the dustpan and climbed back in the chair.

My eyes roamed the room and stopped at the Mack Truck calendar. Miss July, in shorts and a blouse that didn't leave much to the viewer's imagination, was reclining on the fender of a 1950 Mack, red cab, black fenders, an air horn mounted on top of the cab, and of course the bulldog hood ornament. Really cool truck. Wait. Why Miss July? It should have been Miss June. Benny Angelone was murdered in June, not July. Who had changed the calendar to July, and why?

I walked over to get a closer look. It was one of those calendars where you don't rip off the page at the end of a month. Instead, you folded it up over the top, probably to encourage you to collect an entire year of Mack Truck pin-ups. However, someone had torn June from its rightful place between May and July. The tear was irregular, as if someone had been in a hurry.

Had Benny Angelone written something on the back of June, and ditched it because he was sure someone was close to finding it?" I went back to my seat on the barber chair. The missing month could have an ordinary explanation: a customer had a thing for Miss

June or the Mack Truck. I wiped the sweat from my face on my sleeve. And yet, after accidentally finding the notes Benny Angelone had rolled up in the window shade, I thought it reasonable that he might have written something so incriminating, so unimpeachable that proved the guilt of the guy and concealed it in plain sight.

If it had been Benny Angelone who tore off Miss June, might it still be in this room? But where? The waste basket! The bottom was lined with hair and a couple of used neck tissues, nothing else. I was running out of places to look, and I had to take a leak so bad my back teeth were floating.

A heavy thump came from Niedermeyer's. I darn near wet my pants! If Ernie decided to unlock that door and come in here, I was a dead duck. I headed for the door to Angelone's apartment as quickly and quietly as I could and barged into a big wicker basket of dirty towels and Benny's soiled smocks. Somehow I kept it from toppling, but the hinged lid flew open, spilling a bunch of laundry on the floor. I started stuffing it back into the hamper when I saw a crumpled ball of paper wedged between the side of the basket and some towels near the bottom of the hamper. I grabbed it and got the heck out of there without finishing the clean-up.

After shoving the paper inside my shirt, I ran all the way home. Dad's car wasn't in the driveway. I darted in the side door and up the steps to the toilet between the kitchen and the living room to relieve myself.

Mother was pushing the vacuum cleaner in the living room, and the motor noise had covered my hasty entrance. Before exiting the toilet, I took out the paper and unfolded it. There was Miss June in all her glory. I turned over the page and there in Benny's handwriting was a list of names!

Without a warning, the door to the toilet opened and there stood Jimmy. "Hey, I gotta go," he announced. "You're done, aintcha?"

"Yeah, Squirt. Don't forget to flush, and turn out the light, too." He spotted the wrinkled paper.

"What's that?"

"If I wanted you to know, I'd tell you. Just do what you came in here to do." I put the paper back inside my shirt and walked into the living room. Mother had moved into the dining room, and I made it upstairs without her seeing me. Jeannie was not in her room, thank goodness, so I made it to my bedroom and closed the door.

I pulled down the hinged front of the desk. Using it as a desktop, I smoothed out the page as best I could. There wasn't much time. I knew Jimmy would let Mother know I was home. Eleven names were on the list but nothing else. I had hoped Benny would provide some explanation of why these eleven men were listed, but there was nothing. Just the names:

 Gus
Anthony Pino
Vinnie Costa
Joe Specs O'Keefe
Joe McGinnis

Vinnie Geagan
Tom Richardson
Adolph Jazz Maffie
Henry Baker
Jimmy Flaherty
Barney Banfield

As I looked at the names, something jumped out at me. One name didn't include a last name: Gus. I rubbed my earlobe. Why had Mr. Angelone identified this one guy only as Gus? Either Benny didn't know Gus's last name, or he knew Gus well–well enough to be on a first name basis. I looked at the names again. Wait a second: that name O'Keefe: why did that name ring a bell?

"David!" Mother's voice penetrated through the closed door. Nuts!

"Yes, Mother?"

"Your father will be here soon. Time to get ready for supper."

"Okay, Mother. I'll be right down." I put Miss June and the eleven guys in a drawer, closed the desk and walked to the stairs at the end of the hall. As I reached the first floor, I suddenly remembered why the name *O'Keefe* seemed familiar.

I moved quickly to the coffee table where I had last seen the story about the Coudersport bandits. It wasn't there. The paper wasn't on the floor, or in the magazine rack. That news story had been in Wednesday's paper. Mother always picked up the old papers and tossed them in the garbage can. Sometimes she wrapped the supper garbage in yesterday's paper. Mother was in the kitchen, snapping green beans.

"Hi, Mother. Say where did th–"

"What happened at the district attorney's office this morning?" she interrupted

"Don't you want me to wait until Dad gets home?" I asked.

"You're right. That would be best."

"Mother, do you know where Wednesday's paper is?"

"You mean the one with the article about the arrest of the men who robbed Rosenbloom's?" she asked. "I saved it because I wanted to read it again and write a letter to Mabel about it. It's on your Dad's desk."

"Thanks, Mother."

"Why do you want to see that particular article, David?"

"No particular reason. Just curious, that's all. I saw it when I handed the paper to GrandDad, and I told myself I'd like to read it, seeing as how your cousin works in the store that was robbed."

"It's on the desk. Don't mess up any of your dad's papers." Mother had cut the article from the paper. Sure enough, Joseph O'Keefe was one of the Coudersport bandits. His nickname was Specs. Which was how Benny had listed him. The other Coudersport robber was Stanley Gus Gusciora! *Gus*! Gus was the first name on Benny's list! Specs and Gus, convicted of robbery and sitting in jail: somehow they were connected to the other nine names on Benny's list.

One thing for sure. They weren't members of a Sunday School class. I tapped my finger on Gus's name. It seemed I had read that name in a different context. I couldn't recall where or when.

The back screen door banged. Dad was home. He told Mother he had sealed the deal with Dunkirk Radiator, so he was pretty happy, as we all were. Would this parental happiness take the edge off their reaction to what I was about to tell them? I sure hoped so.

After we finished supper and the dishes were washed and put away, Jimmy and Jeannie watched television while the three of us sat at the kitchen table. Dad closed both kitchen doors. I played around with the salt and pepper shakers, mentally rehearsing what I would say. To my surprise both shakers slipped from my hands and crashed to the floor.

"For heaven's sake!" Mother exclaimed. "It's a wonder they didn't break. Stop fooling around and tell us what happened at the meeting."

"Sorry."

"Give them to me. I'll put them out of your reach."

"Mr. Barnes?" Dad prompted.

"OK. Well, he's a very nice man. I'd say he's about your age. He wore a bow tie that he tied himself, which impressed me. I never did learn how to tie one, which isn't a surprise, remembering how much trouble I have with tying knots of any . . ."

"You're stalling. Quit it," Dad said. "Get on with it."

"You're right to be irritated, Dad. I thought you would want some background on . . ."

"David!"

Neither parent said anything until I finished telling them what had been going on, but they made up for their silence. Dad led off, blistering me for lying to them, and for not telling them what I had been doing. Mother nailed me for sneaking into Angelone's.

"Who do you think you are, mister? Your father and I never would allow you to go into somebody's house without their permission." It was no use to remind Mother that there was no way Benny could give me or anyone permission to go inside his place. "You should have let the police handle those things."

The discussion moved to what I had found about the Everett Brown killing, the possibility that Pelinski and Washington were responsible and the close calls with the black Cadillac. Their anger evolved into concern for my safety.

Dad made the final speech. "David, you've been reckless. What possessed you to take things into your own hands? You should have told us about this right away so we could get the authorities involved."

They decided that until Mr. Angelone's killer or killers were caught, my leash would be short. I protested, but my position had become untenable. I knew there was no way my parents would change their minds.

I retreated to my room as soon as feasible. I grabbed paper and pencil and copied the list written on the back of the Miss June calendar page; added an explanation of how I got the list along with the clues about who may have shot Benny Angelone. Next, I wrote a letter to Judy. She really thought things through, and she was trustworthy. She would handle what I was asking her to do and ask no questions.

Dear Judy,
How are you? I am fine, and the family is too. I bet you are surprised that I am writing a letter to you, since I have never done it. The reason is that the Benny Angelone thing has taken a strange turn, and I need your help. Since we talked when you were up here on the 4th, lots of stuff has been happening, not all of it good. Someone, probably the guy who killed Benny Angelone, tried to kill me twice. Obviously it didn't work (ha-ha). This made me mad, and scared, too. So I've been snooping around to find out what Angelone's killer thinks I know. I snuck into the barber shop twice. The first time I found a ~~curios~~ curious coded account of Benny paying lots of money to two people identified as P&W. Then later P&W start paying Benny lots of money. To make a long story short, I did research and got some good evidence that P&W are Pelinski and Washington, the two detectives who questioned Dolores and me. GrandDad advised me to take it to the district attorney, which I did, and now his office is investigating them. I think they're in trouble.

Anyway, I went to the library, and after reading something that I think has a lot to do with Benny Angelone, I went back into Angelone's shop. In the sealed envelope is a list of names I found in the barber shop. I am 90-100 percent sure I know who murdered Mr. Angelone and in some weird way these names have a connection to his death. It's too complicated to tell in this letter, but trust me, this is a big deal.

I have not told Mother and Dad about finding these names. They stuck me deep in the doghouse on account of what I've been doing the past couple of days, and if they found out that I went back into Benny's place I might as well change my name to Fido. *Please don't say anything to your parents!* You are the only one I really trust with what's in the sealed envelope. I don't want to scare you, but what I found out could be dangerous. So, Cuz, if something bad happens to me, then and only then take the envelope to the Pittsburgh office of the FBI. If all goes well, and I feel sure that it will, then I will write next week and ask you to send back the sealed envelope. I promise you that I will let you in on this as soon as I think it's not going to be dangerous for you to know.

Sincerely,
David

I needed Judy's address. Mother had a Christmas card list stowed in a basket of yarn in her bed-room. I don't know why she kept it there; the import-ant thing is I knew she did. I tip-toed through the hall. The sound of Les Brown and His Band of Renown playing "Tuxedo Junction" came from Jeannie's room. Mother and Dad were downstairs listening to the radio. I slipped into their bedroom and grabbed the list and zipped back to my room in the nick of time. They were climbing the stairs as I closed my door.

Saturday morning after breakfast, Mother, Dad, Jeannie, and Jimmy got into the car for the weekly trip to the Twelfth Street Market. I begged off, saying I wanted to read P.G. Wodehouse before it was overdue at the library.

"You stay inside until we get back," Dad com-manded.

"Can I go outside to read?"

"That's fine. See you in about two hours."

Standing on the front porch, I watched the car drive up Euclid until it was out of sight. Dad kept a bunch of postage stamps in his desk drawer. I took two just to be sure I had enough postage and put six pennies in the box. Even if I wasn't being honest with them about my plans this morning, at least I could pay Dad for a couple stamps. I didn't like lying to my parents, even though I did it often back when I was in high school. It's just that they trusted me and when-ever I broke that trust they felt terrible, as if they had failed as parents. If this worked out the way I hoped, I expected that what I was doing behind their backs would be really good for all of us in the future.

  With the letter in one hand, and P.G. Wodehouse's book in the other, I cut through the vacant lot at the corner of Fourth and Sanford, on my way to the mailbox in front of Strubles. I wondered what Judy's reaction would be when she read this letter. I pulled open the letter slot and dropped the envelope down the chute. There could be no turning back now.

  As I turned around from the mailbox, Donny Norton walked out of Strubles. I get along with most people, but not Donny. He walked around like a big shot, the rich kid in the neighborhood. He thought he was better than everyone else. Not only that, but Norton was the biggest brown-noser in the world. He wasn't a good student in English, but he buttered up Miss Bachman, the English teacher, like crazy. All the kids in that class knew he passed only because he praised and flattered her all the time. He tried the same stuff on all the good-looking girls, including Dolores, who thought he was just the funniest boy ever.

  When he saw me, he smiled. "Well, if it ain't Dave the neighborhood celebrity," he said all snotty. "Find any dead people today?" Man, he was a jerk.

  "Yeah," I said. "You." I didn't want to give him the time of day and would have walked away without saying anything more, but Donny wouldn't let it go.

  "By the way, Elliott, thanks for ditching Cooper. I've wanted to get something going with her for a long time." That got my attention. He knew it would.

  "What did you say, creep?"

"We've been going out a lot," he smirked. "Not officially going steady, but it's gonna happen. She's a great kisser, ain't she?"

What happened next was really stupid on my part, although it made me feel good right down to my shoes. My fist smacked him between his nose and upper lip. Blood gushed down his chin onto his shirt. Norton staggered backward and nearly fell.

"See how she likes kissing you without your teeth, you no-good jerk!"

He looked at me like I was crazy, and I guess I was a little crazy. I wanted to hit him again, but Mr. Strubles ran out of his store yelling for me to stop or he would call the cops. Besides, my knuckle was bleeding where it connected with Donny's front teeth. Mr. Strubles took him inside to fix him up. P.G. Wodehouse was laying on the sidewalk. I picked him up and headed home, sucking on my knuckle. That punch was for Dolores as well as Norton. She hadn't wasted any time taking up with someone else.

The phone was ringing when I got home. I knew it would be Mr. or Mrs. Norton calling to find out what we were going to do about my treatment of their precious Donny. I didn't count the number of rings, but it was easily more than twenty. When Mother and Dad heard from the Nortons, they would hit the ceiling. I ran cold water on my hand and thought about dabbing it with Merthiolate. Who could say what Donny had been chewing before I socked him? But Merthiolate burned like crazy. I decided to take my chances. I went out in the backyard under the maple, intending to sit on a lawn chair and try to read. Before I had a chance to open the book, I heard a car pull into our driveway. A car door slammed. Then I heard the front doorbell ring. I slipped in the back way and saw Mr. Norton standing at the front door. He punched the bell again, then started banging the door with his fist. From the way he was acting, you would have thought I had killed Donny.

I opened the door but left the screen door closed. He seemed surprised to see me. "I want to talk with your parents. You know why I'm here."

"Yes, sir. I do. They're not at home." In spite of myself I asked him if Donny was okay.

"He has a chipped tooth and a split lip, thanks to you. I just have one question for you, young man. Why did you hit him?" I wanted to say *because he's a brown-nosing creep*. Instead, I said that his son had spoken of my former girlfriend in a very disrespectful manner, and it had offended me. I went on to say I felt obliged to uphold her honor since she was not present to defend herself.

Mr. Norton looked sort of taken aback by my answer, but he quickly regained the upper hand. "I don't believe you," he said, glaring at me. "Donald has been taught to respect ladies and girls. You had no call to assault him. You're fortunate that I didn't call the police. I will be talking with your parents. I'm sure they will see fit to punish you for your dangerous temper." And just like that, he turned, walked to his car and drove away.

I stood there at the front door, getting madder by the minute. No question I had plenty of anger boiling up to go around. I was mad at myself for letting Donny goad me into socking him, I was mad at that stupid creep for moving in on Dolores, and I was really mad at her for going out with him. I had to admit, smacking Donny in the kisser was 'way on the far side of stupidity. But he was asking for a knuckle sandwich.

About an hour later, Dad and the family parked in the driveway. I pushed myself out on the porch and stood by the trunk to help carry grocery bags. Dad handed me two heavy armloads. "Did you finish *Young Men in Spats?*

"Huh? Oh, not quite."

"How'd you cut your hand?" Jimmy asked. Leave it to my little brother to notice.

"I bumped into something. It's nothing."

Everyone pitched in unloading the food from the market, and Mother and Dad stored the goods in the pantry and fridge. Jeannie set the table for lunch, Dad sliced bread for sandwiches, and mother laid out tomatoes, lettuce, cheese, and lunchmeat. I wanted a braunschweiger sandwich in the worst way, but first things first.

"Uh, listen, before we eat lunch, a little problem -- well, not exactly little -- occurred while you were at the market." They stared at me, motionless.

"I don't think this concerns Jeannie and Jimmy," I said lamely.

"What happened?" Dad asked.

"I punched Donny Norton in the mouth."

"You what!? Why was he here at our house?"

"Well, actually he wasn't here. I wrote a letter to Judy and walked up to the mailbox outside Strubles. I started back home when Norton, I mean Donny, came out of the store. He started it; making fun of me for losing Dolores, saying some disrespectful things about her. I lost my temper and hit him."

Jeannie winked at me. She didn't like Norton any better than most of the kids did. Jimmy stood with his mouth open.

"You two sit and eat your lunch," Mother ordered. "Only one cookie each."

Mother and Dad marched me into the sunroom and closed the French doors.

"You've got some explaining to do, mister," mother said.

"Start at the beginning," said Dad. "You said you wrote a letter to Judy? You never even write a letter to your grandparents. What prompted you to write to her?"

"It was something we talked about over the Fourth. She asked me a question that dealt with our conversation, and I promised her that when I had the answer, I'd let her know. I missed the mailman this morning, so I decided to put it in the mail up at Strubles. I didn't think making that short walk would turn out like it has."

"You're right. You didn't think. Your mother and I told you to stay here, and you took it into your head to disobey us. If you had stayed put, this wouldn't have happened. Stay here. I'm calling the

Nortons."

He got to his feet and started for his office and the telephone.

"Harold, let me talk with them. Go have some lunch with Jeannie and Jimmy."

She motioned for me to come with her. I leaned against the door. She sat in Dad's chair and looked up Norton's number.

Mr. Norton answered the phone. He spoke in a loud voice, not enough for me to hear his words, but I had a clear idea of the gist of it. Mother's remarks reminded me of Abraham in the Bible ready to sacrifice his son instead of a sheep or something.

"There is no excuse for David's behavior, Bob," she said. "Harold and I are so sorry he hurt your son. David just hasn't been himself since he discovered that body."

Oh, brother. I wanted to interrupt and say I would have popped Donny any time; Benny Angelone's murder had nothing to do with it. She listened for what seemed like forever, and then she said, "If that's how you want David to pay for his uncalled-for attack on poor Donald, Harold and I will see to it that he does so. Thank you, Bob."

My punishment was to paint the Nortons' front porch after scraping and sanding off the old paint. Let me tell you, if I had known this was going to be the penalty for punching Donny, I'd have made a better job of it. This was turning out to be the worst summer of my life.

CHAPTER 13

David Scrapes By

Monday morning was rainy, and there was the sound of thunder somewhere out over the lake. I thought for sure Mr. Norton wouldn't want me to start on the porch, but he did. So, after breakfast I grabbed a can of putty, a putty knife, rags, sandpaper, a paper bag with a couple braunschweiger sandwiches and walked in the rain down Euclid to Norton's house, which was the biggest and fanciest house in the last block at the corner of Lakeside. One thing I had insisted: when I was working on their porch Donny would not be there, which was agreed to.

Mr. Norton had left for work, but Mrs. Norton was waiting for me with instructions. Man, there must have been fifty coats of old paint on that dang porch, and by the time noon rolled around, my fingers and arms were stiffer than boards. I sat on the porch floor to eat my lunch, watching the rain come down. Those braunschweiger and mustard sandwiches tasted like sirloin steak, I was that hungry. I had packed a banana for dessert, and as I peeled and ate it I wondered how Mr. Barnes's investigation of Pelinski and Washington was going. I hoped somebody from his office had called and wanted to meet with me that afternoon, because I was already sick and tired of this.

I was glad it was raining which meant the kids who lived in that block, Preston, Finster, and Carney, would be inside, instead of standing around asking a bunch of questions as to why I was working my fingers down to the second knuckles for the Nortons. I stood up to get back to work and saw Mr. Weinbrenner on his way to the lake. He'd be looking for wooden floats which sometimes tore loose from the big nets of the commercial fishing boats. During the war when we kids played soldier, we'd put them on a stick like a big corn dog, only we pretended they were hand grenades. You could whip those babies about a mile. When Mr. Weinbrenner was in front of the Nortons, he waved to me, not a bit surprised that I was working there.

"Hi, Mr. Weinbrenner," I called.

"Hi, there David. Kind of wet today, eh?"

"Yes, sir, kinda wet. Are you going to see what's going on down at the lake?"

"Yep. You know me. Always looking for something to fuss around with."

"Yes, sir. Good luck." Mr. Weinbrenner waved and walked on in the downpour. I got back to the scraping and sanding. I said to myself, Mr. Weinbrenner probably knows this part of the Lake Erie shore better than anybody. The stuff he made from driftwood didn't appeal to me, but what the heck, he enjoyed doing it. And he was always nice to us kids.

Just when I thought my arms would just drop off my shoulders, Mrs. Norton came to the door and told me I had put in a full day's work, and I could go home. She thanked me and said she'd see me tomorrow. Wow. I could hardly wait.

The next morning my luck ran out. Bobby Carney and Jerry Finster walked past, eating green apples they filched from Mr. Brebner's trees. They spotted me and sauntered to the foot of the porch steps.

Finster threw his apple core at a stray cat. "Are you scraping paint off Norton's porch?"

"No. Actually I'm busy writing an essay titled, Stupid Questions I Have Heard." I turned back and commenced scraping.

"Why are you scraping paint off their porch?" Carney asked.

I walked to the edge of the porch. "I entered a contest advertised on the rear cover of Popular Mechanics magazine, and I won. I'd like to shoot the breeze with you, but I'll get a huge cash bonus if I finish this job in ten days, so it's back to work."

They were having none of it.

"How come Donny's not doing that?" asked Jerry Finster.

"Norton?" Carney hooted. "I don't think he knows how to scrape dog crap off his shoe." They laughed, and I joined in.

Carney and Finster were heading for Ernie's to buy two pints of vanilla ice cream over which they would pour two Royal Crown Colas.

"Too bad you're makin' all that money, Dave, and can't enjoy a sundae with us," Finster said.

"I like to let the ice cream get soft before I apply

the RC," said Carney.

"Best way is to eat about half the ice cream before you pour the cola," said Finster. "That way you don't risk having the cola bubble over the side of the carton."

They knew how to rub it in.

Most of the peeling and flaking had been above the porch windows. Now that I didn't need the stepladder and could stand on the porch floor, the work went faster. While I scraped and sanded, thoughts about my precarious situation filled my mind.

"You're playing with fire," I muttered. "That stocky guy could have figured I overheard him and Mr. Angelone arguing that day in the shop. He couldn't know for sure, but he wouldn't want to take any chances. I should have mailed that list to the FBI instead of Judy. Why the heck did I think I could pull this off?

What good will the $100,000 reward do if I were dead? I sat on the porch railing and swallowed the rest of my water. I smacked the railing. Mailing that list to Judy was stupid. I had no business getting her into this.

I took stock of what remained of my porch penance. The siding just above the floor looked bad. Thank goodness I didn't have to do the porch floor. Before leaving for the day, I told Mrs. Norton I'd need more sandpaper. She came out and gave things the once over.

"I'll speak to my husband. Please put your tools and rags over in that corner before you leave."

Just where I always put them. I didn't say anything. I wanted to get home and take a bath.

During the quarter mile stretch from Norton's to home my thoughts returned to the murder. Learning that the guys who pulled off the $3 million Brinks heist wore Captain Marvel masks convinced me my barber knew someone who either passed him the names of those guys, or he stole the list. Either way if I could find how Benny was connected, I'd have the evidence needed to prove who robbed Brinks, and the $100,000 reward would be mine.

After supper, Jimmy and Jeannie watched TV, Mother and Dad had divvied up the paper, and I buried my nose in *Young Men in Spats*. I laughed out loud at "Uncle Fred Flits By" but gave silent thanks he resembled no uncle of mine.

"Oh, no!" Mother said. "Harold, Mr. Rykenicker died. His obituary is in the paper. He's been the sexton at church for over forty years."

"I heard he was ailing," Dad said. "That's too bad. I don't think he had any family."

I didn't pay attention to the rest of the conversation. Obituary. Mr. Benito Angelone's obituary! I snapped shut P.G. Wodehouse and headed for the stairs.

Some instinct had told me to cut Benny's obituary from the paper. I took it from my desk drawer. "Erie Daily Times, Friday, June 23. Benito "Benny" Angelone, 50, suddenly, June 19. Mourned by his parents, Anthony M. Angelone and Rose Gusciora Angelone,

Boston, Mass."

Benny's mother's maiden name was Gusciora. Is Stanley "Gus" Gusciora Benny Angelone's cousin?

By Thursday afternoon I had finished the worst part of the job on Norton's porch. Thank goodness it wasn't stinking hot that week. I planned to start the first coat of paint the next day, but Mr. Norton had bought acrylic instead of oil-based paint. He was out of town and wouldn't be able to exchange the paint until Monday, so Mrs. Norton told me to come back Tuesday. Shoot, this job was dragging on longer than events in the Prince Valiant comic strip.

CHAPTER 14

Digging In The Library

Mother and Dad seemed on the verge of saying no to my plan to return my library book until Jeannie came on board. She said she wanted to go to the Erie Library too, making it easier for me to escape purgatory. We boarded the 9:15 bus for downtown. I told Jeannie it would take me a lot of time, but she said that was OK.

"You can buy me lunch at Eata Hamburg Hot Dog across the square."

"Are you eager to get food poisoning? Dad claims there's a pass-through window from Coulter's Dog and Cat Hospital next door." We laughed.

The volunteer at the Help desk led me to the genealogy files. She gave me a brief tutorial on using the Social Security Death Index, census records for Boston, and birth, marriage, and death records. In three hours, I found what I was looking for. Benny Angelone and Stanley "Gus" Gusciora were first cousins.

I found Jeannie engrossed in an anthology of early 20th Century jazz greats. She used her new library card to borrow it.

"Some of this is really sad," she said. "Some of the finest Black talents suffered needlessly from health problems 'cause they didn't have the money to get good care. Take 'King' Oliver. He died of complications from a gum disease. It was so bad he couldn't play cornet again."

I confessed I hadn't heard of King Oliver.

"Well, you're making my point in a way. His given name was Joseph. He was first to use a muted cornet to play jazz, and he taught trumpet to Louis Armstrong."

"No kidding?"

"I thought that would get your attention."

"If you ask me, the Blacks in this fine country don't have it so good now," I commented. "Case in point, everybody knows Marlowe Tolbert's a state champion in the 440-yard dash. How many people know he graduated from East this year with the highest grade point average? Straight A's since Junior High. Did he get an academic scholarship from an Ivy League university? No. He accepted an athletic scholarship to Ohio State. They're gonna get an excellent man, and not just on the track."

Jeannie shook her head. "Not fair."

"Come on, Squirt," I said. "I'll buy you an authentic hot dog. The daily special is Dachshund."

"You're terrible."

That night, accompanied by the faint sound of Stan Kenton's music emanating from Jeannie's bedroom, I put together a timeline of events from January 17th when the Brinks robbery occurred and on through the dates when O'Keefe and Gusciora robbed the stores in Kane and Coudersport; the Saturday I overheard Mr. Angelone and Stocky Guy arguing.

Finding my barber's body. Dodging the Caddy on my bike. Escaping the concrete from the Hammermill overpass. Finding the P&W notes. Giving them to D.A. Barnes. Discovering the list of names in the barbershop. And finally this morning verifying the relationship of Benny Angelone and "Gus" Gusciora,.

Perhaps what I uncovered wasn't a sure thing, but it seemed possible I had come up with the solution to the Brinks robbery. Over the weekend I would compose a detailed letter to the FBI, and in a few months, I'd get the $100,000 reward! I switched off the light and hopped into bed.

The weekend passed, but I hadn't made any progress on the FBI letter. Letter writing wasn't one of my strong suits, as the wastebasket full of crumpled paper demonstrated. There were a couple of interruptions: a celebratory picnic Bobby Russell's family gave in his honor, and Shea and I watched the movie, *Abbott and Costello in the Foreign Legion*.

Monday evening, I still hadn't written the FBI letter. I regretted not knowing how to type. Writing a four-page letter longhand took almost two hours. I addressed a business envelope I snatched from Dad's store of stationery, sealed and stamped it.

Tuesday morning I rode my bike to the Norton porch with a fast detour to the mailbox at Strubles. As I dropped the letter into the box, I heaved a sigh of relief. I allowed myself a moment of satisfaction. Once the FBI guys got hold of the letter, they would round up those robbers in no time.

By the time I got the gallon of paint mixed it was almost 9:30. The wooden step ladder shelf looked rickety. I pushed down on it. No way would it support a full gallon of paint. Mrs. Norton and Donny had driven off somewhere. I rummaged in the garage and found an empty quart can. I washed it real good and poured in some paint. Frequent refills lengthened the time of the work, but I didn't worry about having a gallon of paint crash through their living room window. It was twenty minutes past six when I finished cleaning the brushes and put the paint rags in the garbage can.

As I pedaled onto Euclid, the wind was blowing hard off the lake, and the air tasted like rain. I wondered if District Attorney Barnes's investigation was making progress. It must be going well, because there hadn't been any more attempts on my life. Maybe that stocky character had gone back to Boston. Or maybe Mr. Barnes had rounded him up. I reached our driveway. Out of habit I scrutinized the street. No black Cadillac. No one on foot. The bike stowed in the garage, I shut the door and headed for the back door. Man, I was starved.

CHAPTER 15

David Gets A Ride

I got up early next morning. Uncle Bob's a carpenter, and I heard him tell Dad laying on the second coat of paint demands close attention to your brush strokes and keeping the area you're working on small. That way the paint doesn't dry out before you blend in your next stroke. In other words, it takes longer to apply paint over the first coat. So I made two large Braunschweiger and cheddar cheese sandwiches, slathered on the mustard, wrapped one of mother's mustard pickles in wax paper, and snitched a butterscotch square cookie and an apple for dessert. I filled my old Boy Scout canteen with ice water, grabbed a bunch of rags from the rag bag, and started for Norton's.
At the end of the driveway I looked up and down the street.

"Hello, David!"

"Hi, Mr. Weinbrenner. I'm on my way to Mr. Norton's. Are you going to the lake?"

"Yes. I intend to stay most of the day. Packed myself a big lunch. May I walk with you?"

"Sure, I'd like that. I guess that storm would blow a lot of stuff onto shore."

"I think you're right. Fact is, Mr. Lee phoned this morning. Occasionally he keeps me informed if something unusual washes in on the beach below his place. He said there's an old boat there this morning."

"Boy, that'd be neat to see. Wish I could go with you."

"I expect she'll be there for a time," said Mr. Weinbrenner.

We walked in silence for a while. I liked that neither of us felt the need for talk. I realized Mr. Weinbrenner was like my granddad in this respect.

"I understand your dad's taking a new position in Pittsburgh."

"Yes, sir. We're getting things ready to move. Mother and Dad want to get us settled in our new home in Mount Lebanon before school starts."

"Umm."

When we were at Norton's, Mr. Weinbrenner stood still. He took hold of my shoulder. "When our youngest son Bill was only two years old, he was dying of the Whooping Cough. Your family had just moved in. I doubt if your parents had even unpacked. Your mother found out what we were up against. She was the first neighbor who came, and she applied mustard plasters, and plugged in a heavy gadget made to steam off wallpaper to provide a steady cloud of moisture to help ease Bill's lungs. Don't expect she ever told you she saved our son's life. Martha and I will miss you all very much." He patted my shoulder and walked on. I stayed put, watching him until he turned left on Lakeside and went from sight. I had no idea.

The paint was an obedient child eager to please her father. Move over, Michelangelo. Sistine Chapel ceiling? Ha! By lunchtime, I put aside the stepladder. I sat on the porch rail and demolished my lunch. Back at it. I'd be finished by two at the latest.

I dipped the brush, scraping off the excess on the rim. With the first stroke, I knew the obedient child had run away. Can't be. Same brush. Same can of paint. The brush had become a porcupine, the paint was gray Jello. After thinning the paint with a dose of mineral spirits, I put the brush in the turpentine, and after a search, grabbed a new brush from the work-bench in the garage. It wasn't much bigger than a toothbrush.

I was working below the large front window when the lights went on in their dining room. In a few minutes Donny, his sister and parents began to eat dinner. I had just finished when I saw Norton slyly give me the finger. I wiped up a paint spot on the porch floor, gathered my stuff and took the paint and brush to the garage. As I walked past the back porch, I saw Norton's sneakers on the steps. I looked at them for a couple seconds.

Oh, what the hell. The dark green looked snazzy, especially on the inside of the shoes, the laces and soles.

As I dragged myself up the street, an old '39 Chevy 4-door heading down toward the lake pulled up next to me, opposite the vacant lot where we used to play football.

"Hey, kid," the driver said with a smile, "can you tell me how to get to Lakeside Drive?" He wore a Pennsylvania Gas Company cap and shirt with the name Dolan printed above the pocket. He needed to see a dentist.

"Yeah. It's straight ahead at the end of this street."

"I got a map here. Could you show me where the Lee family lives on Lakeside?"

"The Lee family?" I said. I wondered why the gas company would send an employee to a house without giving him the address. And he could have found their address in the phone book. But I was beat, and my brain wasn't running on all cylinders.

"Sure." I walked over to the car and put my foot on the running board. Before I could look at the map he was holding, all of a sudden, a guy rose up from the floor in the back. He pushed a gun against my right arm.

"Don't do anything funny, kid. Don't look around, don't yell, just get in the back seat right now and close the door." I didn't argue. The guy driving put the car in gear and drove slowly down Euclid toward the lake.

"Get down on the floor," said the guy with the gun. "Not a peep outa you, or you're dead." The gunman lay across the back seat, pointing the gun at my face. Now that I had a chance to look at him, I saw it was the stocky guy I'd seen talking with Benny Angelone. I couldn't take my eyes away from the gun barrel inches from my face. "Please, God, don't let Dad and Mother see the hole in my face!" The car turned left, and I figured we were on Lakeside Drive. "Here," said the gunman. "Turn in."

The ride got bumpy. Pretty soon the car

stopped, and the driver shut off the engine. "Take a look around," he ordered the driver. He got out, closing the door very quietly. I heard him move away from the car. In a minute he was back. "All clear," he said.

"Okay, kid," muttered my captor. "I'm getting out. Don't move a goddam muscle until I tell you." He climbed out the right rear door and stood facing me, the gun pointing right at my head. "Crawl out." I started to sit up and he hissed, "I said crawl, you hear me? Now crawl!" These guys were gonna kill me, and there didn't seem to be anything I could do to stop them. When I reached the door, he pulled my head back and stuffed a rag in my mouth. Both of them grabbed my arms and pinned them behind my back, shoving me toward the lake. My legs didn't seem to know how to work. The rag made it hard to breathe. "Ain't this where you did Benny?" the driver asked. "Shut up, stupid," commanded the man with the gun.

We struggled through the tall weeds until we were only a couple feet from the edge. The driver let go of me with one hand to push aside a tree branch, and I fought free for a second, pulling the rag out of my mouth. I kind of remember thrashing back and forth, but I wasn't strong enough. I was yelling my lungs out when suddenly there was an awful pain in my head and just before I passed out I was falling in space.

CHAPTER 16

Killer Killed

When I came to, I was lying in a hospital bed. My head hurt something awful, and for some reason, I couldn't take a deep breath without feeling like there was a big, sharp piece of glass stuck between my ribs. My left arm was strapped to my side and there were tubes and bottles all over the place. My ears were ringing, and the room swung in a nauseating circle.

Dad stood at the foot of my bed. When he noticed I was awake, he said, "You're okay, son," like he did when I was little and crying out over a bad dream. This seemed like a nightmare. Then I realized Mother was sitting by the bed, holding my hand. A man stood next to Dad, but everything was blurry and I couldn't recognize him. I felt real sleepy, and just like that I was out like a light.

I lost track of things for the next several hours. When I woke, I couldn't remember anything after the struggle at the cliff-edge. Gradually, little by little, others pieced it together for me.

My doctor said I was lucky to be alive, although with a concussion, broken ribs, broken left shoulder and lots of cuts and bruises, it wasn't like being at a picnic. Every hour a nurse would come in and tell me to cough, which just about ripped my chest in two and made me feel like throwing up. When I told one nurse I wasn't gonna do it, she said, "You have to cough, or you'll get pneumonia." Which didn't seem to be too bad of a trade if I wouldn't have to cough every sixty minutes.

Dad related the most significant portion of what happened. As it happened, Mr. Weinbrenner was walking along the shore as he did most every day. He heard me yell, looked up, and saw the man with the gun and the other guy shove me over. I landed in the lake. Mr. Weinbrenner got to me, pulled me onto the narrow beach so I wouldn't drown, then hurried to the mouth of Two-Mile Creek, which empties into the lake at the pumping station just west of where Benny was murdered. Mr. Weinbrenner climbed up the side of the waterfall, got to a nearby house and called an ambulance and police. Then he came back down and waited beside me until they loaded me in the ambulance. Dad told me that Mr. Weinbrenner was the man standing beside him when I woke up that morning. He saved my life. I started to cry but couldn't move my hands to wipe away the tears. I didn't care. Mr. Weinbrenner was the first person I wanted to be with when I was discharged. And he was.

The Erie police were looking for the two men who'd kidnapped me, but so far, no luck. A policeman– I've forgotten his name–came to my room and asked me if I recalled any threads of conversation between the two guys. I told him the driver had asked the other man if this was where he did Benny.

"Are you sure you heard that right?" the policeman asked.

"Yeah, that's what I heard."

He scribbled something on a notepad. "Thanks," he said, getting up from the chair. "That's important. Excuse me, but I gotta call headquarters."

"Listen, before you go, I have a question that's been bugging me. Why did they throw me off that cliff? I mean, why didn't they just shoot me and be done with it?"

"I'm not a detective, but my guess is they wanted your death to look like an accident. You know, apparently you got careless, lost your footing, and fell. If that man hadn't been there walking along the shore, you probably would've drowned, because you were unconscious, lying in the water. Accidental death. No questions asked. Killers get away with murder."

The cop looked at me for a second. He shook his head. "I read in the paper that the ambulance crew told the reporter they couldn't believe you survived."

Dad and Mother returned to the room. Mother asked if I felt any better, I lied that, yes, I did feel much better. Dad said, "I called Art to let him know what happened, and he wanted you to know he's pulling for you."

"That's nice," I said.

"Funny thing," Dad continued, "Art called back in less than a minute to tell me Judy insisted she had to go to the FBI office in Pittsburgh right away because she had something to give them, something you sent her in a letter. She wouldn't tell Art what it's about. What's going on?"

Judy. I knew she'd come through. A nurse came

in, stuck a thermometer under my tongue and took my pulse and blood pressure, so I couldn't talk for a minute. I wondered how Dad and Mother would react when I told them what was going on. The nurse looked at the thermometer, wrote the results on a clipboard, ordered me to cough, gave me some pills and poured a glass of water.

After she left, I asked, "Did Uncle Art take Judy to the FBI?"

"He did."

"That's good. I have to talk with the FBI right away. It's…"

"Wait a minute," Dad interrupted. "You haven't told us what you mailed to Judy and what that has to do with what happened to you."

"I'll tell you the whole story, honest, but please, first phone the FBI and tell them I have something that proves that the man who tried to kill me also murdered Mr. Angelone. I can show them why he did it, and that his killing is part of a much bigger crime that hasn't been solved yet. I have some information about who did that one, too."

At first they looked at me like I was out of my head, but pretty quick they saw I was serious.

"No, that's not going to happen," Dad said. "You've been seriously injured. You need to concentrate on helping your body to heal. That means doing exactly what the doctor and hospital staff tell you to do."

"And what we tell you to do," Mother added. "You're in no position to tell us or anyone what to do and when to do it. You don't realize what the rest of us have been through. The least you could do for us and for your sister and brother is to forget this other nonsense and get some rest." She squeezed my hand. "Please, son." I held her hand until she gently let go.

I dozed off again, and when I opened my eyes it was dark outside. Neither Mother nor Dad seemed to be around. A nurse was writing something on the chart. I noticed she was kind of good-looking, which must have meant I was feeling a little better. The nurse–ironically her name was Dolores–brought me a fresh pitcher of water and poured a glass. "You're quite the celebrity," nurse Dolores smiled. "There's a policeman sitting outside your door. I think they're afraid you'll try to escape from us."

"You're kidding. Really, there's a cop on guard out there?"

"Really. So don't try anything funny." She laughed, patted my arm, and went out, closing the door. She had forgotten to tell me to cough. Her omission was like finding a million bucks. The feeling didn't last. Her words about the cop worried me. The police wouldn't guard my room unless they thought I might still be in danger. It didn't worry me enough to keep me from falling asleep again.

I don't know how long I'd been sleeping, but suddenly I was awake. In the semi-darkness I noticed movement. The door was closing. A doctor wearing a white coat walked quietly toward my bed. He was holding something in his hands. I raised my head. A pillow. I didn't want another pillow. Before I could tell him so, he lunged, pressing the pillow over my face! I twisted my head away and got my right arm under his, but he was too strong for me, and clamped the pillow tight over my nose and mouth. I tried to yell, but I was running out of breath. All of a sudden his body yanked backwards, and I could breathe and see. The guard had pulled him off me and was trying to throw the attacker to the floor, but he was having a tough time of it. The room light blazed. The guy in the doctor's coat was the one who threw me off the cliff! Another man rushed in to help, but the assailant wrenched free from them and ran out into the hall with the guard after him. There were shouts and screams, and the sound of people running, then BLAM-BLAM! Someone screamed, then it got as quiet as a church.

The man who had helped fight off Stocky was a real doctor. He went to the door and peeked around the corner real careful. "It's the guy who tried to smother you," he said, breathing hard. "The cop shot him. He's on the floor at the end of the hall. I have to help." He hurried out. A nurse ran past the door, pushing a gurney.

In about ten minutes, the doctor came back.

"Is he . . ."

"He's dead." He checked me over. I was breathing hard, and every breath I took was so painful I darn near passed out. Nurse Dolores came in, and they hooked me up to some oxygen to help me breathe easier.

"The nurse will give you a shot to put you to sleep, Dave," he said in a calm way. You've had more than enough excitement." Nurse Dolores swabbed my right arm, jabbed the needle in and that's all I remembered until the next day.

While Mother helped me eat breakfast–cold toast, over-cooked eggs, weak coffee–she told me that to get the cop guarding my room away for a few minutes, my assailant somehow got a doctor's coat and told the guard there was a call from the police station waiting for him at the front desk. My barber's killer came darn close to killing me. Mother said *The Erie Daily Times* reported that police identified him as Dominic Montevecchio, a convicted felon who lived in Erie. According to the paper, Dominic had a long record of violent crimes.

There was a brief knock on the door frame. A tall man wearing a blue suit and maroon tie walked in.

"Good morning," he said, all business. He pulled a badge from his coat pocket. "I'm Agent Max Glasser with the Federal Bureau of Investigation District Office in Pittsburgh. My office received an envelope yesterday delivered by persons who identified themselves as your uncle, Arthur Elliott, and his daughter Judith, your cousin. Miss Elliott said she received this envelope in a letter from you last week. Can you verify this?"

"Yes, sir. I sent her the sealed envelope."

Agent Glasser placed my copy of Benny Angelone's list of names on the bedside table. "Tell me how you came to possess this." So I related how I found the list stuffed in a clothes hamper in Mr. Angelone's shop. When I finished, he took the list and put it in his briefcase. "Your efforts have resulted in uncovering some very interesting information," Mr. Glasser declared. "Thank you for your service." With that, the FBI agent prepared to leave.

"Excuse me, sir," I said. "May I say something?"

Agent Glasser got this exasperated look on his face as if to say, *Listen, kid, I've got more important responsibilities than spending time listening to you.* No question about it, his attitude was off-putting. Here I was, lying in that hospital bed, pretty well busted up because I found out what the police and FBI hadn't, and he was going to walk out without listening to what I had. Glasser made a show of looking at his wrist watch as if to say, *okay, but I don't have all day, so make it brief.* He remained standing.

"First off, I believe Benny Angelone was murdered because he was told by one of the men named on the list, Gus to be exact, that these eleven guys robbed the Brinks garage in Boston last January. Then Benny tried to use this information to blackmail the head of the Brinks gang, but the gang leader gave the order to have Benny Angelone killed instead."

Max Glasser sat. "What gives you that idea?"

"Well, it all sort of came together when I overheard Mr. Angelone tell Montevecchio he knew all the characters in the Captain Marvel story. That made no sense to me until I read the newspaper story about the Brinks robbery and how the robbers wore Captain Marvel Halloween masks. I went back to the barber shop and found the list of names. Judy gave you that copy. I thought I recognized one of the names, so I reread three news stories in the Erie paper: Mr. Angelone's obituary, and two articles about two men who robbed a couple stores in Pennsylvania. Sure enough, one of the guys arrested in Towanda, Pennsylvania was Joseph "Specs" O'Keefe, and his name's on that list. The other Pennsylvania robber was Stanley "Gus" Gusciora, entered as Gus. Further research disclosed Benny and Stanley Gusciora are cousins.

Agent Glasser leaned forward, forearms on his knees, hands clasped. He looked me straight in the eye. " The FBI has been investigating the Brinks robbery since the day after it happened. I can't share anything about the scope of the manhunt the bureau is conducting, except that every lead, all tips we receive, are thoroughly pursued. The individuals on the list you stumbled on are criminals known to various Massachusetts police departments and the FBI. Boston newspapers reported a few weeks ago that Mr. Pino, who is on your list, was questioned by the Boston bureau and provided a solid alibi. Mr. Angelone could have listed those individuals for any number of criminal activities, from stealing money from the offering plate to racketeering." He slapped his knees and stood,

"Be assured that I will personally forward this list to the agents conducting the investigation. If your information proves useful, you will be contacted." Max Glasser nodded to Mother, then shook my hand. "Thank you, David. All citizens should be as conscientious as you."

"Sir, before you go. What if Mr. Angeline's cousin gave him the list because he needed Benny to get in touch with someone on that list, maybe the boss? And if Benny couldn't get hold of him, then he should call another guy. Maybe Gusciora and O'Keefe needed money for a lawyer or had to warn the others that the Towanda cops were suspicious. They wouldn't dare telephone the gang leader. Or, Gus gave Benny those names as an insurance policy. What I mean is, if the boss decided Gus and O'Keefe needed to be killed to keep them from spilling the beans, Gus could tell him that someone else had the names, and if anything happened to either him or Specs, the names would be given to the FBI."

"I don't want to cut you off, David, but the conjectures you've come up with have been considered and checked out by teams of highly-trained professionals with years of experience in these cases. Believe me, if any of those theories held water, the bureau would have the perpetrators in custody."

Max Glasser pushed back his shirt sleeve to see his wristwatch. "Sorry, but I have to leave." He addressed Mother. "Mrs. Elliott, the original list of names David found is evidence in this investigation. I'll have to take it with me. May I arrange to retrieve it later today, or tomorrow?"

"With all due respect, Mr. Glasser, you have the copy of that list. The original isn't necessary until the guilty parties have been arrested and go on trial. However, David needs to retain the original to claim the reward the Brinks Company has offered for anything that would help solve the robbery."

"The copy won't suffice as evidence," he declared. "Besides, as I mentioned, the story your son just told doesn't prove these names are connected with the Brinks robbery."

"Mr. Glasser, what David has uncovered may give the FBI a lead. After you question these individuals backed up with the facts David uncovered, the Brinks robbery might be solved. I think David has good reason to keep the original in his possession. And as I said a few minutes ago, if and when those who robbed Brinks are apprehended, convicted, and brought to trial, I assure you we will give you the original list on the reverse side of the calendar. But until then, we're going to keep it with us."

"Mrs. Elliott, I don't want to make this difficult for you. If you don't voluntarily relinquish the paper I requested, I will get a court order to obtain it."

"Well," said Mother, smiling up at him, "I suppose that's what you'll have to do. Now, David needs to rest. He's been overdoing it this morning. Goodbye, Mr. Glasser."

"Agent Glasser," I jumped in, "if the list doesn't have anything to do with the Brinks gang or Mr. Angelone's murder, why did Montevecchio make multiple attempts to kill me?"

He went out without giving any answer.

As soon as he left the room, Mother stood and walked to the door. "I'll be back. I have to call your Dad to alert him not to give your list to that man."

Agent Glasser did try to get Dad to give up the

Miss June page that day, but Dad told him he wouldn't turn the list over to the FBI without a court order. Dad said later he figured Glasser would be standing at the courthouse door when it reopened on Monday. Dad photographed both sides of the calendar page and took the film to Strubles to get it developed. At least we would have a complete copy of the original to offer the Brinks Company in return for the reward.

CHAPTER 17

Life Isn't Always Fair

One afternoon a week or so after getting pushed off the cliff, I was sitting in a chair in the hospital room, reading *Riders of the Purple Sage*, a Zane Grey story GrandDad had sent me. Dr. Lawson walked in. We had a nice visit, although he wondered why I had abruptly quit mowing his lawn. Luckily, he didn't press me on it. He gave me an envelope, a get-well card from Cynthia, which I didn't open until he left. The card smelled faintly of her perfume and she had written a thoughtful note. I kept that card until the end of my freshman year in college.

Dolores Cooper visited me in the hospital, too. Her eyes showed that she was shook seeing me lying there like a trussed-up sausage. Dad left the room so we could talk. I asked her what was going on in her world. Mr. Strubles had hired her to dish ice cream and run the cash register after the other girl quit. She said her sister had just started dating a man who worked at GE.

"How about you, Dolores? Are you and Donny dating? Going steady?" She looked away for just a second, and I knew they were. It didn't really surprise me. Just before she said goodbye she leaned over and kissed me. I thought about saying that was better than kissing Donny, but I didn't.

Shea came to visit two days after my shoulder surgery. He said he would have to reconsider being my friend, since I was hanging out with such dangerous people. We were having a great visit, talking baseball and such. But the nurse asked him to leave because he was making me laugh, which still brought on unpleasant reminders that the ribs weren't completely healed. Both of us realized we wouldn't have time to get together before I moved, but we pretended we would.

"Tell you what, when they give you your "'Get Out of Jail Free' card, we'll eat lunch at the Parade Street "Ptomaine Palace," and have some of those greasy square hamburgers like we did when we were playing for Sementelli's."

"You're on," I said. "And we gotta order their limp-as-shoelaces French fries. Unless the Board of Health has finally closed them down."

On his way out, Shea paused in the doorway and gave me a thumb's up. "See you later, Ellie," he said. "You'll be good as new in no time." Friends like Shea don't come along very often. I missed him already.

That was six years ago. Needless to say, a lot has happened since then. Pelinski and Washington were convicted and sentenced to long prison terms for killing Everett Brown and framing Willie Wilson. I testified at their trial, and my testimony helped in a small way to strengthen the district attorney's case against them. Knowing I had played a part in bringing them to justice and getting Willie Wilson out of prison gave

me a lot of satisfaction. However, there was no satisfaction coming from the investigation of the men
whose names Benny had written on the calendar. I'm
talking about the 1950 Brinks robbery which just got
wrapped up this past January.

Back then, when I was still in the hospital my
family and I thought for sure the Boston police and
the FBI, armed with the list of names I had found on
that calendar page, would round up the Brinks criminals in no time. We thought I would get the reward
for helping to solve the crime. However, that's not
what happened.

Max Glasser, the FBI agent, did get a court
order, and we had to give him the original calendar
page. I don't know what he did with it, but neither it
nor my persistent communications to the FBI got to
the right people.

Not that it did me any good, but the men
Benny Angelone named on the back of the Miss June
calendar page turned out to be the Brinks gang, as
I had deduced. I handed Glasser the solution to that
crime on a silver tray. Either he or somebody else
messed it up.

Not only that, but Gus Gusciora and O'Keefe
were in prison at that time. How hard could it have
been to question them? Yet in spite of all this, the ali-
bis of those eleven robbers were never broken by the
Boston police or the FBI. For a couple years my family
and I believed that any day those guys would be arrested, and Brinks would pay me the $100,000.

On the two-year anniversary of the robbery, I

made an anonymous phone call to the FBI in Boston telling them the names of the guys on that Miss June calendar, hoping that would back up the information I had given to Glasser. But nothing happened until earlier this year. Then, just a few weeks before the six-year statute of limitations expired on January 17, Joseph "Specs" O'Keefe met with FBI agents and told them everything. O'Keefe named all eleven gang members. He detailed how Tony Pino cased the robbery site and how they executed the theft, from the first planning meeting to the getaway.

One of my theories as to why Gus Gusciora asked Benny Angelone to meet with him while he and O'Keefe were in jail over in Towanda proved to be correct. I speculated that those two crooks needed money for a lawyer. It turns out Gus and Specs did need money to pay attorney fees. Benny was supposed to call Tony Pino and tell him to wire money to the jail. But Benny decided to blackmail Pino by threatening to go to the FBI with the names he got from his cousin. I guess Benny thought Pino would pay him at least twice the amount of the reward for keeping his mouth shut. A fatal decision by Benny, that's for sure.

After Pino had Dominic "Stocky Guy" Montevecchio kill Angelone, Montevecchio apparently told Pino he suspected I knew Benny was talking about the Brinks robbery when I overheard him talking about Captain Marvel. I can still remember Benny's words: "I know the names of all the characters in the Captain Marvel story." Pino and Montevecchio didn't know for sure I had figured things out, but Pino couldn't take a chance, so he ordered Montevecchio to kill me and make it look accidental. He nearly pulled it off.

I doubt that I'll ever find out what happened to the evidence I sent. Did someone at the FBI drop the ball, or did the list get lost in the massive number of leads the bureau received? The astonishing thing is they were questioning most, if not all, those crooks at the time. If it hadn't been for O'Keefe confessing and implicating the rest of them, they might have gotten away with it. From the newspaper accounts and the FBI report which recently became public information, not much of the stolen money has been recovered yet.

I can't help thinking occasionally how life would have played out if someone in authority had believed me. That $100,000 reward would have made life easier for my family and me. I guess once Specs spilled the beans, Brinks decided they didn't need to pay the reward to anyone.

When the story that the Brinks robbery had been solved aired on the television news, Shea called me from Chicago wanting to know how I felt about all this. "Shea, I feel like I pitched a no-hitter but lost the game on a bad call by the first-base umpire."

In the intervening six years, I have experienced the normal -- and not so normal -- events of living. I fell in love with Judy, my cousin. Not so normal, until we found out she's not my cousin. But that's another story. Last year, 1955, I graduated with a Bachelor of Arts degree from Passavant College, where I played on the baseball team for three years until I re-injured my shoulder. I majored in American Literature under a wonderful professor who taught his students much more than the creative wisdom of Whitman, Melville, Twain, Flannery O'Connor and Zora Neale Hurston.

During my college years, I mulled over what I wanted to do for the rest of my life, or some portion of it. Two or three possibilities pulled at me: teaching literature, criminology, and law enforcement, specifically becoming a detective. The pull toward teaching was the natural consequence of the influence of Stephen Jeffrey, my American Lit professor. In some strange way I think Professor Jeffrey was, at center, the reason for my nagging ambivalence about a teaching career. I admired him immensely, but doubted I had the passion and the commitment to literature he had evidenced.

Criminology and law enforcement held an interest because I like to work on solving puzzling questions about incidents and people. All three of these career ideas meant more years of education and first-hand experience. That's par for the course in any career if you want to be good at it.

I got plenty of well-meaning suggestions from family and friends. One particular suggestion got me: "David, you're a good leader, an excellent listener. I've watched you handle differences of opinion between members of a student group, even on the baseball team. You know exactly how to smooth things over. I think you'd be an outstanding cement finisher." Seriously?

After doing research and asking questions of

reliable individuals I decided not to pursue any of the careers that had appealed, not even cement finishing. Those who knew me then had the good manners to not laugh, pass out or argue when they learned I have embarked on the vocation of an ordained minister of the Lutheran Church. This September I became a first year student at the Lutheran Theologian Seminary at Gettysburg. The courses are difficult, not surprising since seminary curriculum is graduate school level. My ideas about the Bible, Lutheran teaching and Jesus are undergoing a radical change. The circle of friends I've made at the seminary say the same is true for them.

This year has not been all fun and games. In January, an extraordinary man who led me through a terrifying time of my life died a tragic death. He had a tremendous impact on young people. The next month my Dad died suddenly of a heart attack. I still can't accept it. Why did he think he had to work such long stressful hours? For what? For whom? Jean, Jim and I were heart-broken messes, but Mother was a wreck. In those days before, during and especially after Dad's funeral and burial, I suddenly realized I had never truly known my mother. That epiphany moment shook me to the center of my being. As we walked away from the grave, this huge door opened in my mind, and I saw myself standing on a shore, looking out at an empty, glass-calm sea. As I stood there, I understood I did not really know any of my immediate family: not my sister, not my brother, not even Dad. Then the door closed, and I was sitting beside Mother in the funeral car. For the first time since the phone call telling me Dad had died, I wept.

ACKNOWLEDGEMENT

Who can write a book without utilizing the amazing resources of a library and the equally amazing professionals, the librarians and the always helpful volunteers? My special thanks to the Erie Public Library. From its former location on Perry Square it has become a treasure trove of the latest in communication technology while retaining the hands-on expertise and personal help that makes a library wonderful.

To Kerry Staply, my superb editor who works with me like ham works with eggs. It's a pleasure to team up with you, Kerry. Thanks for all you do to improve my writing, especially by cutting the philosophizing.

I am thankful for the memories I have of my coming-of-age neighborhood on the far east side of Erie. To all the kids I played and fought with and their families, thank you for what you have given me.

Thank you most of all, Karen, my intelligent loving friend, fellow-traveler, adventurer, alpha reader, book formatter, confidant.

ABOUT THE AUTHOR

Bailey Herrington

Bailey Herrington hails from western PA. Born in Pittsburgh, he lived
in Erie during his school years. After
completing studies at The Lutheran
Seminary at Gettysburg, Herrington
served churches in PA and WV for
24 years. In addition to writing
weekly sermons, he created his "al-
tar" ego, "Pious Pete the Protestant
Pope," using humor and satire to
poke fun at the foibles of the organized church and
Herrington himself.

A Writers' Digest Short Story course taught him to
revise and hone plots, characters, and scenes. Bailey says, "Had I taken the course at the start of my
ministry, my sermons would have been better – and
shorter!"

A friend challenged him to write a murder mystery
based on a kumquat. "The K Factor" suffered the fate
of most first attempts at fiction, but the writing bug
had bitten deeply. He has written and published via

Kindle Direct Publishing three mysteries based on actual crimes: What the Barber Knew, Dead to Rights, and Pack of Scoundrels.

His fourth book, The Girl in the Orange Maillot, will be co-published by Koehler Books, February 28, 2022.

Bailey lives in Las Cruces, NM with his wife Karen, striving to be a better writer, and a better person.

PRAISE FOR AUTHOR

The teen-aged main character, telling his story in first person, is very funny and charming. The mystery in the story is solved rather rapidly at the end of the book, and seemed a little far-fetched for a hero of that young age. It was almost an afterthought, as the most appealing part of the book is the musings of this "old-fashioned" teenager in 1950. Reminiscent of Nancy Drew mysteries, I think this most would mostly appeal to young adults.

- WILDONE

If this is his first published book, I am really looking forward to what Bailey Herrington comes up with next. This is a refreshing voice in the mystery genre. David Elliott, the hero, is so authentic. He IS a teenaged boy of the 1950's. What he does, what he eats, his fights with his brother and sister and what he thought of world topics all evoke the age and pull the reader along in the story. The action moves briskly and soon we find ourselves a bit worried about what is going to happen next. But David keeps plugging along on his quest for the truth, except, perhaps when he has to tell his parents what he is doing. You will enjoy reading "What the Barber Knew" and will be asking for more.

- CURLY

What a fun read! It's hard to believe that Bailey Herrington hasn't been published before now. His attention to detail, of the era and location, is spot on. You can feel the heat radiating from the summer sidewalks and smell the Lake Erie breezes! The main character, David Elliot, is the perfect storyteller with his youthful point of view, exploring what's important to a seventeen year old boy as well as being driven by a strong set of values. Ultimately, when confronted with life's curveballs, he steps up and goes yard!

Repeat after me.... Sequel!

- REISLING

This book was a real page turner, and very entertaining!!! I am so happy I purchased this book, look forward to the next book from the author. Way to go!!! Please get us another book out to read SOON!!!

- PATRICK

BOOKS BY THIS AUTHOR

What The Barber Knew

David Elliott, adventurous high school junior, stumbles upon the murdered body of his barber, Benny Angelone. Days later David narrowly escapes death at the hands of an unknown assailant who believes David heard or saw something that will send the barber's killer to the chair. He tracks young Elliott's every move, looking for the moment to strike. But what does Elliott know? What did the barber know which signed his death warrant? In a desperate race against time David must find the answers or be killed. His daring efforts involve him in one of the most famous crimes of the 20th century and bring him - and the reader - to the cliff's edge with a relentless killer.

Dead To Rights

David Elliott's major professor Steven Jeffrey dies unexpectedly. The next day David receives a mysterious coded letter from him. Elliott's attempts to decipher the message thrust him into a tangle of intrigue, murder and peril, masterminded by a cadre of U.S. government agents. At all costs these operatives must prevent the stunning facts of the professor's death from being revealed.

As David fights against those who want to kill him, he also struggles with personal attitudes and beliefs which risk the loss of friendship and love.

Judy Elliott, David's cousin, proves to be a resourceful, intrepid partner, and surprisingly much more. How will these cousins respond to what they grow to realize about themselves and each other? Will they prevail against powerful enemies of individual rights and the rights of a democratic society?

Pack Of Scoundrels

Las Cruces, New Mexico. 1954. The suspicious death of a friend and a Confidential memorandum stolen from the epicenter of America's postwar space program plunge young David and Judy Elliott into a deadly battle. They must uncover the real name of the mysterious "Cholla" to find the key that unlocks the answers to their friend's death, the memo and the unsolved murder of a teenager.